KT-219-403

Also by Shirley Barrett

Rush Oh!

'Who would have thought horror-humour would be so fun? It's chilling, but so camp and perfectly paced that it works'

Elle

'It defies convention. I was hooked from the opening pages ... it's laugh-out-loud horrible and perfectly nuts – you'll never find anything like it again'

Guardian

'This is a sharp, twisted, hilarious treasure of a book. Sort of *Twin Peaks* meets *Bad Teacher* that had me laughing, wincing and falling in love with the flawed and flawless narrator'

Jess Kidd

'Ingenuously exploits folk horror conventions ... Funny and harrowingly honest'

Toronto Star

Shirley Barrett is a screenwriter, director and novelist. She lives in Sydney, Australia. Her first novel, *Rush Oh!*, is also published by Fleet.

'Bursting with raucous energy, while anchored in seriousness, *The Bus on Thursday* is an intoxicating horror-humor romp'
Jeff VanderMeer, author of *Annihilation*

'Barrett's brilliant second novel plummets headlong into a darkly funny tale'
Mail on Sunday

'Funny, angry, feminist ... [Barrett is] a masterly world-builder'
New York Times Book Review

'[Eleanor] is an entertainingly sardonic companion on this blackly humorous journey into horror'
Observer

'This quirky tale is thrillingly original and wildly funny. A slippery narrative keeps you guessing what's really going on with a sharply witty narration'
Sunday Mirror

'[A] bonkers, rather brilliant comedy ... Savagely funny, *The Bus on Thursday* takes the nineteenth-century literary conceit of a woman going mad in the face of repressive social expectations and updates it with brio for the twenty-first century'
Metro

Bromley Libraries

30128 80405 171 5

'Shirley Barrett has crafted a quirky, one-of-kind, wild ride of a novel with demons, kangaroos, a missing school teacher, a remote town where things are strangely off-kilter, and a wonderfully bizarre cast of characters. *The Bus on Thursday* is a darkly funny and deeply unsettling novel you'll devour in one sitting'

Jennifer McMahon

'Fast, funny and downright weird, but a great read'

Woman & Home

'A darkly funny story in the company of a riotous, jinxed heroine'

Psychologies

'Barrett's narrative rushes headlong forward in a crazy and exhilarating rush of emotion and plot ... I fell head over heels for *The Bus on Thursday* for its plain bonkers plot'

Stylist

'This quirky tale is thrillingly original and wildly funny'

Sunday People

'Hilarious ... This witty, wise and rather demented novel occupies a strange, and possibly unique, space between screwball comedy, murder mystery and magical realism'

Wendy Holden, *Daily Mail*

'It's a hilarious tale, and Eleanor is the perfect anti-heroine. One to brighten gloomy afternoons'

Image magazine

the
Bus
on
Thursday

Shirley Barrett

FLEET
2019

FLEET

First published in Australia in 2018 by Allen & Unwin
First published in Great Britain in 2018 by Fleet
This paperback edition published in 2019 by Fleet

1 3 5 7 9 10 8 6 4 2

Copyright © Shirley Barrett 2018

The moral right of the author has been asserted

*All characters and events in this publication, other than those
clearly in the public domain, are fictitious and any resemblance
to real persons, living or dead, is purely coincidental.*

All rights reserved.
No part of this publication may be reproduced, stored in a
retrieval system, or transmitted in any form or by any means, without
the prior permission in writing of the publisher, nor be otherwise circulated
in any form of binding or cover other than that in which it is published
and without a similar condition including this condition being
imposed on the subsequent purchaser.

A CIP catalogue record for this book
is available from the British Library.

ISBN 978-0-7088-9880-2

Typeset in Bembo by M Rules
Printed and bound in Great Britain by
Clays Ltd, Elcograf S.p.A.

Papers used by Fleet are from well-managed forests
and other responsible sources.

MIX
Paper from
responsible sources
FSC® C104740

Fleet
An imprint of
Little, Brown Book Group
Carmelite House
50 Victoria Embankment
London EC4Y 0DZ

An Hachette UK Company
www.hachette.co.uk

www.littlebrown.co.uk

For Kate D

I was at work scratching my armpit. I was literally at my desk scratching my pit and I felt it and I freaked out and I didn't tell a soul and normally I'm the kind of person to blurt out everything. So I guess I panicked from the word go.

I had the mammogram first. I had several mammograms because they couldn't get to it—it was in a really awkward spot. Also, apparently I was not relaxed enough. My not being relaxed enough while they flattened my breast like a hamburger patty and blasted it with radiation was causing them problems. They kept hauling out interesting new attachments for the mammogram machine, like it was some kind of fancy-arse Mixmaster. They were asking me questions like, 'Are you on the pill? Have you missed any pills?' And I was on the pill, but I'd been really slack about it because I'd broken up with Josh and I wasn't seeing anyone. But this woman kept insisting I be precise. 'What do you mean, you missed a day? How many days did you actually miss? Could you be pregnant?' And she was sweating, there were literally beads of sweat breaking out on her forehead, so I knew.

1

They did a fine needle biopsy next. They said, 'Anaesthetic or no anaesthetic?' I said, 'Give me the anaesthetic, both barrels.' They said, 'Word of warning: having an anaesthetic needle stuck in your breast is every bit as excruciating as the actual procedure. Possibly more so.' I said, 'Give me the anaesthetic anyway, I'll take my chances.' I was trying to be brave, you see. Which was pointless. Let us draw a veil over the fine needle biopsy.

Next they left me alone in a cubicle for a while. When they came back, they said, 'Okay, the fine needle biopsy was inconclusive'—i.e. complete waste of time, sorry for the fact it was excruciating—'so we're going to try something now called a vacuum-assisted core biopsy. Have you ever had one of those before?' Let me just say, if I had had one of those before I would have taken my cue to run screaming from the building, but instead I just shook my head meekly and followed them into the torture chamber. 'Word of warning,' they said, as I climbed up on the rack, clutching my hospital gown around me. 'This will sound a little bit like we are going at your breast with an industrial staple gun. Also, it will feel like you've been kicked in the chest for no reason by a champion rodeo bucking bull.'

I kid you not.

Well, they didn't actually say that, but they should have.

Anyways, I got to have three goes on that ride because the first couple of rounds were 'inconclusive'.

After they scraped me down off the ceiling, I went back in to see the doctor. She'd obviously decided the best approach was to speak very briskly and firmly about cell reproduction. And I'm just sitting there staring at her because I had literally no fucking idea what she was talking about. So she drew this helpful diagram on her notepad, indicating how nice cells reproduce (neatly) and how my cells were reproducing (lots of random crazy circles piling up on top of each other). Then she says, 'I'm sorry to say you have breast cancer.'

I'm like, '*Whaaaat??*

The fuuucckk??'

Then I'm like, 'Aren't I a little on the young side to have breast cancer?' I guess I hoped this might be what you call mitigating circumstances. I guess I was angling for a reprieve or a reduced sentence or something, but she didn't even blink.

'I've had younger,' she says.

Then she says, 'You've got an appointment with the surgeon at three o'clock.' And I'm thinking, *Wow, this is quick.* And then next thing I'm thinking, Wow, this surgeon looks exactly like George Clooney—George Clooney back in his *ER* days—and also, this surgeon likes to get around in his scrubs a lot because it makes him look even more like George Clooney back in his ER days. And somehow having my surgeon look exactly like a handsome movie actor just made everything worse.

Because ordinarily, under normal circumstances, exposing my breasts to a man who looked like George Clooney and having him stare at them intently and then fondle them (sort of—more prodding and kneading, actually), this would be a very pleasurable swoon-worthy experience. But given the fact that he was about to knock me out cold and go at my breast with a carving knife (scalpel, whatever), let me just say it wasn't. Also, his hands were cold and he made no attempt to warm them. Also, his interpersonal skills were not tremendous. He seemed to think that if he was even one per cent charming or warm or sympathetic, women would just completely fall in love with him, so he compensated for his sensational good looks by having zero empathy and being very direct, very clinical, like he didn't have time for any nonsense. He says, 'It's an aggressive tumour, and we've got to get it out.'

No sugar-coating the pill with George Clooney.

He doesn't believe in it.

Long story short, I have a lumpectomy.

And you know what? It's not too bad. Hats off to George Clooney. There's a neat little incision, and my breast still looks pretty much like a breast. Slightly less stuffing maybe, but if I pulled my shoulders back and stuck my chest out, it still looked pretty reasonable. So for the first time since the day I scratched my armpit, I have a flash of hope. I think, Well, maybe I'm going to get out of this relatively unscathed.

Ha.

A week later, I go back to see Mr Clooney. He says, 'The margins weren't clear; you've got mutations around the outside of the specimen.' I'm thinking, *Mutations around the outside of the specimen??* Where does he get this language? Could he possibly make me feel any more of a freak? Is there not a better word than 'mutations' (plural), especially used in same sentence as 'specimen'? And then he says to me very calmly, like he's playing a doctor in a TV show, 'We're going to go back in and take a little bit more.' And at this point I'm still hopeful that I might emerge from all this with a breast that doesn't look like it's been cobbled together by Dr Frankenstein, so I say, 'How much exactly?' And then he gets this odd look on his face like he hopes this will sound reassuring but he knows in advance that it won't, and he says, 'Just the right amount.'

Which was pretty much when I realised that these guys haven't got a clue—they're basically just winging it. George Clooney's plan in a nutshell was this: lop a bit more off and hope for the best. And of course, I've got no choice in the matter; I've just got to go along with it and hope for the best also.

So I have another operation, and my breast is starting to look a bit wonkitated now, a bit sad and deflated like a beach ball after the dog's been at it. But I'm trying to be upbeat, because of course being a good cancer patient is all about being positive, and a week later I go back to see George Clooney and get the results. And he says, 'Well, I've taken twelve cubic centimetres from here right down to behind the nipple, and the margins still aren't clear. So this is what we have to do. You'll have chemo now, and at the end of that, you'll have to have a mastectomy.'

And I'm just going, *Fuck*.

Mastectomy.

Because that was the one word I absolutely did not want to hear.

Chemo—who cares? Hair grows back, so do eyelashes. Breasts, on the other hand, do not. In casually dropping the m-word the way he did, George Clooney was basically wiping out my femininity, my sexual desirability, my ability to look at myself naked in the mirror—everything. He might just as well have said, 'Oh, and by the way, you'll never have a husband, you'll never have babies. It's doubtful whether you'll even have sex again.' I felt sick. Sick to my guts. I had exactly that sick horrible doomed feeling you get when they push the safety bar down into lock position on the Wild Mouse at Luna Park. That's the best way I can describe it. That's exactly how I felt.

Meanwhile, before the chemo and the body-part removal, I had to go off and be a bridesmaid. My BFF Sally was getting married and naturally she turned into a fucking Bridezilla. She was like, 'Never mind your cancer, are you still gonna be my fucking bridesmaid?' Seriously, that's how she talks. So I had to buy the hideous dress which cost $600; I had to fly to Orange for the kitchen tea which cost $250; and supposedly she was going to throw in for the shoes, but then she totally backed out of the shoe deal. Plus, all the bridesmaids had to pitch in for the candy-apple KitchenAid so she could sit it on her benchtop and never use it, even though she kept promising to bake me cupcakes. (What is it about breast cancer that makes people think of cupcakes? Oh. Right.) So basically Sally wiped out the small amount I had in my bank account. And I'm about to quit work because teaching is not the kind of job you can do when you're sick on chemo. That's when I literally had thoughts of becoming a nun, because I figured, well, I'm never going to have sex again. If I became a nun, I would at least have somewhere to live. Because I'm seriously thinking, What the fuck am I going to do now?

All the way through chemo, with the hair falling out and the mouth ulcers and the night sweats, I'm still thinking there has to be a way I can get out of the mastectomy. I was in denial, of course; I see that now. Not meaning to brag, but my breasts had probably been my best feature. Josh had been obsessed with them—ironically, we used to have enormous fights if I wore anything too low-cut. But more than that, the thing that really bothered me was the actual act of them slicing it off—it just seemed so barbaric, so macabre, like some kind of medieval punishment. I remember thinking,

Well, what do they do with it? Where does it go? How do they dispose of all these body parts? And then the whole idea of this imitation breast, this thing that only does impersonations. So even when I pick up the phone to book the operation, I'm still thinking, There has to be a way out of this. It can't be the only way.

Anyway, I make the call and I go back to see George Clooney, and I say to him, 'Listen, do you really, really believe I have to do this?' And he got extremely angry with me. He said, 'Eleanor, you can bury your head in the sand all you like, but if you don't do this, you'll be back here in two years, you'll have lymph nodes involved, you'll have chemo again, and it'll be everywhere.' He said, 'It'll be fun and games for two years, then you'll be back here.'

Fun and games for two years. So I had the mastectomy.

Wow. I reread all that and I think, Who is that angry person? What's with all the smart talk and the swearing?

That's because I hadn't yet started weeping. The weeping followed shortly after, and lasted maybe twelve months.

What started the weeping was Sally getting pregnant. Because of course Sally gets pregnant straight away, like I mean *straight away*, on the actual honeymoon in Vanuatu. Here's how I found out: her Instagram feed. In among the beach sunsets and the bikini martinis and the breakfast buffets, there's a shot looking out through the billowing muslin curtains of their fashioned-from-driftwood four-poster bed. Sheets conspicuously entangling a bare foot, still with bridal nail polish. Outside—like smack outside, they could not be any fucking closer—the pristine turquoise waters of their tropical paradise.

Caption: Moment of conception #perfectbliss #lovedup #misterandmissus #nofilter

To which I respond: No fucking filter, my arse.

Now, I have known Sally since year five taekwondo, and I am well aware that she is the most fiercely competitive person I have ever known—also, she is 9th Dan in the Art of Casual Cruelty. And yes, some would argue that she and Brett had been together almost six years and she is past thirty now, so no surprise that she gets herself knocked up immediately post-nuptials. But still, something about the timing of it bothered me.

Not to seem like a crazy person, but if the situation were reversed, and my best friend was dealing with a breast cancer diagnosis with all its resulting uncertainty about her reproductive future, I think I would hold off on the 'Baby Makes Three' shit for a year or two.

But that's just me, I guess.

I mean, Sally was actually sitting right next to me, when Doc, my beloved oncologist, was explaining the whole chemo vs babies thing to me. He's like, 'So, do you have a steady partner?' And I'm like, 'Sadly, no.' And he says, 'Well, we could freeze your ovarian tissue blah blah, but given you're so young, I'm hopeful you'll be able to conceive naturally after treatment.' And I'm like, 'What do you mean, "after treatment"?' And he says, 'Well, you've got six months of chemo, then your mastectomy, then five years of tamoxifen, which is some kind of fancy hormone suppressant.' And I'm just going, *Are you kidding me??* Given I'm even sexually viable after all that, I'll be thirty-six years old with crow's feet and spider veins and approximately one and a half eggs left per ovary—seriously, what are my chances? And meanwhile, all through this, Sally is stroking my arm and making warm empathetic noises and having the absolute time of her life playing doting best friend to tragic cancer victim, entirely for Doc's benefit. I mean, Doc actually said to us as we were leaving something about me being lucky to have such a good friend, and Sally bats her eyelashes and says, 'Ever since year five taekwondo. She threw me so hard I ended up in a back brace for six weeks.' And then she goes, 'Fighting spirit, Doc. If beating cancer's all about fighting spirit, Eleanor's got it licked.'

I mean, please.

I could have decked her all over again, then and there in Doc's office.

The fact is I took the reproduction stuff hard because that was a big part of the reason why Josh and I broke up. He suddenly announced one day that he didn't want children, and was I fine with that? Well, no, I wasn't fine with that, Josh, and I especially wasn't fine with the way you only just saw fit to mention this to me after four years as a couple, joint bank accounts and numerous white goods not to mention a ludicrously overpriced home cinema purchased together. Even notwithstanding major household appliances, I have invested a lot of time and energy into the relationship, and now I am standing here with egg on my face, excuse pun. And he's like, 'Well, I just assumed you already knew this about me', and it's true, he was always reading gloomy books about overpopulation, but I just dismissed this as Josh being an egghead eco-warrior (why does the word 'egg' keep coming up when I write about this??). So anyway pretty soon after this conversation, we break up. And next thing, I'm sitting in Doc's office realising that maybe I'd never be able to have kids anyway, which struck me as bitterly ironic. Laughed at by the gods, as Amy would say. (I played a lot of Amy Winehouse during the break-up.)

Anyway, looking back, I freely admit that I may have sunk into a bit of a depression. Which is of course completely normal after breast cancer. After all, I used to have a life, a job, a boyfriend who adored me, two exceptional breasts and a one-bedroom apartment in Annandale. Now, I'm an unemployed thirty-one-year-old living with my mother in Greenacre. With one remaining original breast and a kind of phony-looking, slightly too perky silicone lump alongside it. And yes, I sound extremely negative and I get ticked off about this constantly, especially by Mum, but the fact is, I'm just being realistic. My life has changed, and not in a good way. Yes, I am cancer-free, but look at me—what reasonable person wouldn't feel a little down in the dumps?

But I've been to see my GP about that, so I'm all sorted now, pharmaceutically speaking. And you know what? I really feel like I'm starting to turn a corner. My hair is beginning to look half-decent. I've started exercising. I've started looking for work a bit more seriously. I've started going out and seeing people again. And this week, I've only had one major crying jag, and it's Friday. So I'm doing good.

This is what caused my crying jag: I went to see Doc for my three-monthly check-up. I freely admit that I am pretty much in love with Doc, even though he is fifty-seven and balding and looks like your uncle. Actually, to judge from the waiting-room conversations I have overheard, everyone is in love with Doc because he is kind and gentle and has warm hands and is extremely good at his job, but I like to think I have an extra-special relationship with him because I am one of his younger patients and I call him 'Doc' and make jokes, and he thinks I'm hilarious. Sometimes I have even fantasised about us getting together. Which is totally weird, but also probably totally normal.

Anyway, he seems really pleased to see me—my scans are all clear, everything's rosy. And we chat about this and that, and I tell him my periods have started up again, and that I intend to celebrate this by getting knocked up by the first guy I see. And then I suggest (jokingly, of course) that maybe Doc is the man for the job because I could certainly use some brains in the gene mix. And he laughs and goes red (adorable!) but then gets all sombre and says, 'Seriously, Eleanor, I do not want you falling pregnant just yet. Have you been using contraception?' And I say, 'Doc, I am not an idiot, if a miracle happens and praise be, I get to have sex again, well of course I would use contraception.' And then Doc goes on about how when I finish my five-year course of Tamoxifen, I will still be young enough to get pregnant safely so that gives me a few years yet to meet my dream guy etc. etc. And I say, 'Yes, but my dream guy would be a cross between Bruno Mars only taller and Doc, and seriously what are the odds of such a mythical creature existing, let alone me bumping into him in Greenacre?'

And then we get on to the nightmares I've been having and how the Tamoxifen may or may not be causing them, and he says, 'Well, what are the nightmares about?' And I say, 'What do you think they're about? They're about the cancer coming back, of course.' And he says, 'That sounds like anxiety to me, Eleanor. How about you check in with the counsellor or go back to the support group?' And I'm like, 'Are you kidding me? After last time?' And then his phone beeps with obviously some kind of prearranged cue from his secretary and he glances at it and makes an apologetic face, and I realise he's trying to think how he can wind things up with me so he can see his next patient, on account of the fact that as always he is double-booked. So I say, 'Are we finished?' in a kind of offended voice. And he says, 'Unless there's anything else you need to ask me?' So I say, 'Well, when do I see you again?' And I realise that I sound extremely needy, and not appealingly patient-in-distress needy but actual bunny-boiling psycho-stalker 'Play Misty For Me' needy. So he says, 'Come and see me in six months. Book an appointment with Liz on your way out.' And here he puts his hand on the small of my back, because (I realise now) what he is actually doing is ushering me to the door. But I'm absolutely gutted that I don't get to see him for six months, and I'm interpreting his hand on my back as him subconsciously conveying that he's gutted also. So I say, 'Am I still your favourite patient?' trying to sound jokey but actually sounding desperate and pathetic. And by now he has his other hand on the door handle. And he smiles at me and says, 'Always,' and as he's opening the door, I lunge in to kiss him. That's right, I *lunge*. For the lips. And he deftly moves his head just in the nick of time so I kind of connect with his jaw, but not before everyone in the waiting room has witnessed the entire thought-provoking spectacle. Of me lunging at Doc. And him ducking to avoid it. So I bolted.

Started crying in the lift, which was chock-full of interested bystanders. Realise amid my tears that because I am coming from Oncology, everyone assumes that I've just been given six weeks to live, because they keep throwing me compassionate glances. One nice lady surreptitiously opens her handbag and passes me one of those mini-packs of tissues, which I accept, feeling fraudulent. Little does she know that I am crying because I just lunged at a balding, paunchy fifty-seven-year-old who feels sorry for me at best and rebuffed me. Continued crying all the way home. Went straight to my room and cried for another four or five hours. Refused dinner, then got up later after Mum had gone to bed and ate an entire packet of chocolate biscuits from Aldi.

Lesson to be drawn from this: *No more lunging.*

On the bright side, he did say, 'Always.'

Why blog? Good question!

To which I can only respond: Well, it is better than scrapbooking. These were two of the suggestions offered at the breast cancer support group I went to once and one time only. Those poor buggers whose cancer has metastasised got nudged toward the scrapbooking table. If they are nudging you towards the scrapbooking table, then it is basically code for, 'You will die soon, so quick! Throw some photos in an album as a keepsake for your loved ones. Make sure you are smiling in these photos and have lots of hair. Decorate with butterfly stickers and inspirational quotes about dancing like nobody's watching etc.'

What is wrong with me? Where does this horrible snarky voice come from? I have actually met women in exactly this predicament, desperately trying to stay well enough in their few remaining months to put a scrapbook together so their young children won't forget them, hoping that they'll flick through it from time to time in years to come and be reminded how much their mother loved them and how horrible it was for her to die and leave them so young, and here I am being a fucking glib fucking smart-arse about it.

16

The worst thing the thing that scares me most about this voice that jumps out whenever I attempt to blog anything about this experience—is that this smart-arse funny angry shit is exactly how everyone's breast cancer blogs start. Before it starts getting worse and the news is bad and the latest scan shows a lesion on the liver and the posts get fewer and fewer till finally some friend or husband or mother gets on and lets us know that Amy or Genevieve or Susie finally lost her brave battle, passed away quietly, another angel in heaven, another star in the night sky. But they all start off with the funny-angry voice, and it's exactly what mine sounds like right now, and that scares the shit out of me.

One thing for certain—I am definitely keeping this private. There is no way I am uploading any of this to the internet. Why the fuck anyone would go public with this shit is beyond me.

Still no job. Even though there is apparently a chronic short-age of teachers and a crisis in education to judge from the news reports. I am beginning to think about retail or even, God forbid, hospitality.

Here's why I never went back to my breast cancer support group.

First, let me just say upfront, I am not at my best in a group-type situation. Generally speaking, I am the surly one in the corner, snarling if anyone tries to pat me. My problem apparently (according to Sally) is that I act like I'm better than everyone else, which I am not, so I give off hostile vibes. Truth be told, I was just really profoundly pissed off at finding myself there, and who wouldn't be? Slumped on a beanbag surrounded by fifteen middle-aged women in aggressively cheerful headscarves, smiling bravely through their tears. Another thing, there was just way too much laughter and hugging, like cancer gives you licence to be zany. Seriously, it was painful.

The theme of the evening was 'My Cancer Journey', and that alone should have given me pause since all journeys have a destination, cancer journeys in particular, and it's not a destination anyone had any intention of talking about. Instead, we were each invited to bring an item of some description to express something 'meaningful' about our experience so far. Here's what some of the others brought: a beautiful card from husband, expressing his love for her; a hideous wig to be donated to third-world cancer charity as hair now growing back; scan results showing all clear; a photo of three children hugging (bald) Mummy.

Here's what I brought: a docket from the David Jones lingerie department, where that same afternoon I had been refused a refund on two underwire bras purchased some eighteen months earlier.

'Have you worn these?' asked the sales girl, fingering the bras doubtfully.

'Yes, I have, repeatedly,' I said. 'They gave me cancer. See? No hair.'

Here I pointed helpfully to my headscarf.

'Well, if you've worn them, we can't give you a refund.' She didn't give a shit about the headscarf.

Unpleasantness ensued. To be honest, I pretty much lost it. There was shouting (me), also tears (me). The point I was trying to make was that if DJs insisted on peddling known carcinogens for profit, then the very least they could do by way of compensation was give me a fucking refund so I could buy myself a pair of caramel suede ankle boots I fancied over in Footwear. A measly $139.98, that's all I wanted. Was that going to break the bank? Or would they prefer I go to Slater and Gordon and rustle up a class action because, believe me, I would be more than happy to get cracking. Anyway, long story short, I was asked to leave by security, and on the way out I sent a rack of nighties flying down the aisle, narrowly missing an elderly customer. They let that one go, they were so happy to see me out of there.

So as I said, this incident had happened that same afternoon, and I was still feeling a little shaken up about it. I mean, I knew I'd behaved badly, and the whole underwire bra link to breast cancer is tenuous at best, and basically this had all arisen out of me being too broke to afford the boots I coveted. But still, I thought, you know what? The fact remains that I did get breast cancer, and *something* most certainly gave it to me, so why not the lingerie department of a large department store? And on my way to the support group, realising I had forgotten to bring along anything 'meaningful' about my cancer 'journey', I thought, well, maybe I could share the experience with the group, because at the very least everyone would likely sympathise with me, and possibly I could even get to the point of having a laugh about it.

Ha.

They came down totally on the side of David Jones. They all thought I was nuts too.

'Underwire bras do not give you cancer.' This from the counsellor, of all people.

'I'm not saying they give you cancer in general,' says me. 'They don't give you bladder cancer or testicular cancer. But I'm talking specifically about breast cancer.'

Shouted down by the entire group, all apparently armed with the latest research.

'And also, I'm sorry, but having cancer is not an excuse to be rude to shop assistants,' said Fright Wig for Africa, a shop assistant in her former life. Wife of Loving Husband Who Finally Penned Nice Card After Twenty-five Years of Marriage was appalled, hygiene-wise, that I had tried to return used underwear, except instead of saying 'used underwear' she kept saying 'soiled underwear', and I kept having to reiterate that both bras were perfectly clean as I'd gone to the trouble of washing them. Someone else couldn't understand why I didn't simply put the boots on lay-by. Others felt that although it was legit to play the cancer card in returning unwanted merchandise, in this instance I had overplayed the cancer card and thus made it harder for everyone else to score concessions from major department stores by deploying their bald heads.

Blah blah blah blah.

When they'd finally finished, I said, 'You know what? I'm actually sorry I mentioned it.' And then I said, 'Are you sure this is a support group? Because I don't feel like I'm getting a lot of support here.'

'Eleanor, I feel you need to give yourself permission to acknowledge you may have some unresolved anger issues,' said the counsellor.

'You know what? I'm giving myself permission to get the fuck out of here,' I said. And that was the last time I went to breast cancer support group.

So I went on a date. The first proper date since I broke up with Josh and got cancer.

Sally set it up—it was a guy from her work. She's been getting impatient with what she calls my whole 'Oh poor me, I had cancer' thing. She's like, 'Yes, but you're better now and your hair has grown back, so can we talk about something else for a change?' This is pretty typical of Sally; she is very no nonsense and calls a spade a spade—i.e. she is totally lacking in empathy. Also, she believes I have created a shrine for Lost Love—i.e. Josh—and I am going to end up like Miss Havisham if I don't kick the shrine over and get on with life (her words).

Anyway, she's been telling me about this guy at work called Harry, who is long-term single and no one can understand why because he is the greatest guy ever and also, btw, drives a Lexus. The other small detail about Harry which she finally got around to mentioning is that he has a cleft palate. Well, he's had the surgery, but you can tell there's been some work there. So I guess Sally's reasoning was this: guy with funny lip plus girl with funny boob equals Romance.

And in fact, I actually thought Harry was kind of cute. He's one of those guys who thinks, Okay, well, I'm a bit on the fugly side, so let's make up for it with lots of personality and a great sense of humour. Because he was fucking hilarious! Also, he had a really nice body. Anyway, we met at the Coogee Bay for a drink, except I'm not really drinking these days, so I just had one glass of wine and he meanwhile got pretty hammered because he was nervous, which was kind of endearing. I myself was extremely nervous—I'd been stressing about it all week. I spent the entire day giving myself beauty treatments, and actually had to wash my hair twice because I totally stuffed up my first attempt with the curling tongs and basically frazzled all the ends. Also, Mum bought me a new dress from Iconic, which was sweet of her—it was on sale so only $59, and I have to admit I looked pretty damn sexy in it.

Anyway, so Harry and I get on like a house on fire, and seriously he made me laugh more than anyone I've met in a long time, and that was nice because there hasn't been a whole lot of laughs in the last year or so. And although I'd agreed under duress to go on a date with him, I didn't seriously ever contemplate that I would end up in bed with him or anything. Because I'm so totally not ready for that yet. I mean, I still don't have a nipple. But anyway, we actually started kissing, tongues and everything, while we're still at the pub, and then he says, 'Do you want to come back to mine?' And I really, really like the guy so I say, 'Well, okay . . . '

So we get back to his apartment in Bronte, and he makes me a cup of camomile tea and then we start seriously getting it on, right there on the sofa. And we're pulling each other's clothes off and all the while I'm thinking, *Does he know about the fake boob?* Because he seemed to know I'd had cancer, but I wasn't sure how much detail Sally had gone into on the subject. So we're making out and he's having a good old grope and I'm thinking, Well, maybe he knows and he's fine about it, because he sure seems pretty enthusiastic. I mean, he was all over the fake boob along with the real boob, and so far, so good, like he hadn't recoiled with horror or anything. And by now I've got my top off and he's undoing my bra and then the next thing he puts his head down between my tits and then he freezes. Like he literally freezes. And he says, 'What the fuck's going on there?'

That's right: *'What the fuck's going on there?'*

Those were his exact words.

And I say, 'Oh, sorry, I thought you knew, that's my fake boob, it doesn't have a nipple yet. Sorry, I should have warned you.' I actually apologise (twice!), can you believe that???? The reality is, in spite of the apologising, I was actually feeling really fucking angry. Because in all honesty, this guy was a very, very ordinary kisser. It was all just way too wet and slobbery, possibly because of the cleft palate thing, possibly not, but my point is I didn't think to complain about it. I was absolutely prepared to put up with it, to make

26

allowances, because I thought he was such a great guy. But obviously he was not prepared to make allowances for me. Because he went off the boil immediately, by which I mean that he sat right back on the couch and said, 'Whoa. Whoa,' like I'd turned into a rattlesnake. So I immediately put my bra back on and, in my desperation, start undoing his pants and fishing my hand down there, but he pulls me off and says, 'Oh, I've had too much to drink. I don't think I'm going to be able to get it up.'

Really, it doesn't get much more humiliating than that.

So I got dressed and hot-footed it out of there. He basically hid in the bathroom till I'd gone.

Anyway, next day I text Sally: *Thanks a lot. Completely fucking humiliated by Harry the Harelip.* And she obviously gets the lowdown from him the minute she gets in to work because she rings me up mid-morning and says, 'Harry is really sorry—he was just totally thrown by the no-nipple thing. Also the scar. Like, he's super apologetic and he says he thinks you're fantastic, but maybe because he's had so much surgery himself, that sort of thing just freaks him out.' And then she has a go at me for not getting the nipple done, and hence bringing this whole thing upon myself. And then she ticks me off for calling him Harry the Harelip, which she said was offensive.

I hung up on her.

Firstly, I am really, really upset that she is discussing me, her supposed best friend, in such intimate detail with this insensitive fucking prick. Probably over the coffee machine in the kitchen, with anyone else who wants to join in and trade horror stories about unpleasant surprises in the bedroom. Second of all, I am furious at her for setting me up with this dick in the first place. How extensively did she actually vet this creep before throwing me, her supposed best friend, at his mercy? And lastly, how fucking dare she have a go at me about my nipple?!

So the deal with the nipple is I have to have it tattooed on, and then they do this needlework to pucker the skin up and make it look sort-of-kind-of-not-really like a nipple at all. I mean, would any sane person think that sounded like a happy solution? And yes, I will get it done eventually because I have no better option, but let's face it, would the needlework nipple have passed muster with oversensitive Harry and his delicate sensibilities? I absolutely doubt it because Harry, like all guys, expects perfection.

I'm so angry with Sally, I'm just going to cut her off for a while. This whole thing has set me back emotionally six months, just when I was starting to feel strong again. Not to mention confirmed all my fears about dating.

I keep having these twinges. In the right breast, near the armpit, around where the lump used to be. Just these strange, sharp little twinges that send a kind of shudder right up my neck and around the back of my skull. I don't like it. I keep thinking, *What's that? Is that the cancer spreading?*

Can you feel cancer spreading?

And a few days ago in the shower, in the *other* armpit, I felt a tiny lump on one of the glands or tendons or whatever the hell those cordy things are. (Lymph node? Could that be a palpable lymph node? Palpable's bad, that much I know.) But weirdly I haven't felt anything there since, even though I spend a lot of time in front of the bathroom mirror, prodding and poking and trying to find it. And yet I know I definitely felt something, quite distinctly. So where's it gone? And what's that all about?

Here's a tip: Never google *what does breast cancer metastasis feel like*. Turns out it feels like just about anything! Here are some metastasis symptoms I've experienced in the past three days: feeling tired, feeling under the weather, cold or flu-like symptoms, headache, feeling like you've pulled a muscle, tingling sensation in arms, blah blah blah blah blah.

Clearly I am riddled with the fucker.

I have to keep reminding myself that all my last scans were clear. So what's with the twinging? Maybe I should ring Doc up and ask him . . .

So I rang him up and left a message, and good old Doc, he's so fantastic, he gets back to me straight away. And I explain the whole twinging thing to him. (I didn't mention the tiny disappearing lymph node because it suddenly felt a bit ridiculous, and I'm conscious of not wanting to look like I'm just trying to get his attention, especially after the lunging incident.) And he's like, 'How long has this been going on?' And I'm like, 'Maybe a month?' And he says, 'I'm pretty sure it's just your tissue healing itself—it takes a long time after surgery, and patients often experience strange sensations.' And I'm like, 'What tissue? Do I even have any tissue in that breast? Isn't it all just implant?' And he gives me a lengthy, detailed description of what sort of tissue and nerve endings surrounding the implant could be twinging, and finally I interrupt and I say, 'I've just got a bad, bad feeling about this in my gut.' So then he says, 'When are you due in to see me again?' And I'm like, 'Four months.' And he says, 'Well, we could bring you in earlier, but I think we should just see if it settles of its own accord. Let's give it a couple of months.' And I suddenly feel this wave of anxiety that maybe he doesn't want to see me because he's worried I'm going to lunge at him again. So I fall silent. And he's like, 'Eleanor? Are you there?' And I say, 'Yeah, I'm here,' and he says, 'Would you feel better if we booked you in to see George Clooney again and you talked it through with him?' And I'm like, 'No, I do not want to see George Clooney again, he will just want to lop the other one off.' And he laughs, because we always joke about George Clooney and his terrible interpersonal bedside skills.

And then, I don't know what possessed me, but I suddenly blurt out that I'm sorry I lunged at him at my last appointment, and I hope he didn't think I was just dreaming up excuses to come and see him and lunge at him again, and he says, 'Of course I don't think that,' and I say, 'I really am twinging, I'm not just pretending I'm twinging,' but somehow the very fact that I say this out loud makes it seem like that's exactly what I am doing, and finally I am so struck by how tragic and needy I sound that I hang up on him.

So of course, good old Doc, he calls me back right away. And he says, 'Are you doing okay, Eleanor? Emotionally? I'm just a bit concerned about you.' Whereupon I immediately burst into tears as I always do whenever anyone's nice to me. And he says, 'Do you need to go and talk to your GP again?' which is code for 'up your anti-depressants asap', and I'm blubbering, 'I just want my old life back!' And in the background on his end, I can hear his secretary saying something to him, and I imagine him covering the receiver with his hand and gesturing at her that he has a crazy one on the line (not that he would ever do such a thing) and suddenly I have this vision, this vision of all those women in his waiting room in their headscarves and beanies, waiting for him right now as he tries to deal with me; women who have it in their bones and brains and livers, women who are coming to the end of the line of possible chemo cocktails that will do anything for them, and when they walk into his office and find him staring at their terrible scans, the tumours all coming back, different organs this time, poor harried Doc will have to tell them that he's finally run out of options, and unfortunately he'll have to pass them on to Palliative Care.

I feel so ashamed of myself, I apologise for wasting his time and hang up on him again.

A small miracle, just when I most desperately need it! I have a job, and a kind of dream job, the answer to all my prayers!

So ... the story is that it's a tiny school (eleven students!!!) in a place called Talbingo, miles away from anywhere! I just googled it. Unbelievably picturesque, to judge by the photos. 'In the foothills of the Snowy Mountains, on the shores of the Jounama Pondage ... ' Population—get this—241!!! Except now it must be 240, because the teacher's gone AWOL.

I am not sure why they have so carelessly misplaced their teacher in the middle of the school year, but anyway, they need a replacement pronto. Like, they rang me this morning, and they asked if I could possibly get there by tomorrow. I said, 'Tomorrow? I'll be there this afternoon!!' And then I said, 'Just kidding,' because it's actually a six-hour drive away. (Jesus, I hope the Corolla can manage it. It's totally overdue for a service, also the clutch keeps slipping.)

These sorts of events, when they happen, make me almost believe there is a God or some kind of larger force that looks after me. I mean, this job could not be more perfect for me right now. Eleven students. Clean mountain air. How stressful could that be? The best thing is I get my own house! Hooray! (Just tried to see what the house looks like on Google Maps, but failed. It's so fucking isolated, Street View hasn't made it there yet.)

Mum came in just before with some clothes she'd ironed for me, and then she hung around watching me pack, and I could tell she was worrying and I said, 'Mum, I'm going to be *fine*!' And she said, 'I'm just worried you'll get lonely.' But frankly, I am so over everyone right now that I basically can't wait to get away from them all. Except Mum, of course, but she can visit. I mean my 'friends', ironic use of punctuation intended. I'm still not talking to Sally, obviously, after the Harry the Harelip fiasco. And the other night I went to the pub with Fee and Nicki and a few other chicks from school, and Nicki basically said to me, when we were talking about the causes of breast cancer, she actually said to me, 'Well, you have always been a *stresser*.' And I sort of stiffened and said, 'What do you mean?' And she said, 'Well, you know, you just always get wound up over things.' And I know she's saying this because earlier I asked her if she could blow her smoke away from me because it was making me feel ill. So I said, 'You mean, like now? Because you keep blowing smoke in my face when I've just had cancer? What you are basically saying to me is that I had it coming?' And I just got up and walked out of there. She messaged me the next morning, very apologetic, with about a zillion sad faces and xxxxx, and I responded, *No problem forget about it,* with one x and a winky face, but truly I'm so over the lot of them, I really am.

So anyway, I am frantically trying to get my shit together, but I just wanted to take this moment to collect myself and gather my thoughts. Give myself a bit of a talking-to. Yes, I had a spot of cancer, but I am well now and it is time to STOP WALLOWING and look to the future. I have been given this opportunity, the sort of posting I've always fantasised about, even before the cancer, and it's important that I don't succumb to my usual issues, but instead *make the most of it.* Also, try to be more positive, less judgemental about people. Eat healthy, get fit. Also, I'm packing my yoga mat. All that mountain air will be so good for me. I am really going to try to get into some kind of routine with my meditation.

Well, that was awkward! Also a little *weird*.

Okay, so I get here after this six-hour drive, and the last thirty minutes were like the opening titles in *The Shining* except no snow, just kangaroos and lakes and rivers and mountains and the sun getting low and flaring through the windscreen—just all so exhilaratingly beautiful, I could actually feel my heart almost bursting in my chest. And then you come around the corner and there's Talbingo, and sure enough it's this tiny little collection of cottages nestled in the foothills of the Snowy Mountains, and it's dead quiet, like NO ONE around. I mean, it's so small and so deserted that I can hardly believe it actually warrants a school?! Anyway, I find my house no worries, and it's in a prime position overlooking what I think might be a golf course (though I haven't seen any golfers), which in turn overlooks the Pondage, which seems to be a fancy name for a pretty little lake. The house itself is this nice little weatherboard, very plain, very simply furnished, all a bit Nanna but clean and tidy and kind of sweet. Neatly pressed tea towel hanging from the oven. Old-fashioned chenille bedspread on the bed. Embroidered cushion in the living room: *Let your smile change the world but don't let the world change your smile!* Anyway, I'm feeling pretty happy unloading the car, enjoying the mountain air really crisp and cool on my face, when suddenly this woman comes careening up the driveway carrying these shopping bags, and it's Glenda, who apparently works in the office at the school. And she's like, 'Are you Miss Mellett, the new teacher?' and I'm like, 'Yes, but please call me Eleanor,' and she's brought all this milk and bread and stuff, even a chicken casserole for my dinner tonight, which was really nice of her, and she starts telling me how grateful they are that I've come at such short notice etc. etc. And I'm trying really hard to be super friendly, which is part of my new positive life strategy *(let your smile change the world!)*, so I say, 'Come in and have a cup of tea,' and she presses her lips together and shakes her head, then she goes all red in the face and starts to cry.

And she's saying, 'Nothing against you, Miss Mellett, I'm sure you're lovely, but just being here with a *replacement teacher*, it's all very, very distressing.' This is all blubbering through her tears while I'm just standing there like an idiot, holding the chicken casserole. And she's going, 'I'm sorry, I'm sorry, it's just that we all loved Miss Barker so much!', and I'm going, 'Of course, of course, please, won't you have a cup of tea?' and then she shouts, 'IT'S TOO SOON! IT'S TOO SOON!' Like, she literally shouts it at me, and she has a look on her face like she could hit me. Then she immediately launches into this apology which goes on for about five minutes and it's all about how she hasn't been herself since

Miss Barker left etc. etc. and I'm thinking, could we maybe not talk about Miss Barker and how wonderful she was the *entire* time you're supposed to be welcoming me? Anyway, she composes herself a bit and starts telling me about the school, and what time to rock up tomorrow, and then all of a sudden she blurts out, 'I've got all her belongings packed up in our spare bedroom. That's all we have of her—six boxes!—but it's ready—it's ready for her when she needs it!' And then she takes off, like she actually hurtles off down the driveway.

So that was my welcome to Talbingo.

Obviously the wonderful Miss Barker—she who has seen fit to suddenly abscond in the middle of the school term—used to live in this house too. Can I blame the decor on her? Probably not. But someone has certainly been very paranoid about security because there are about a zillion locks on the doors.

Well, my first day went pretty well.

The school is just beyond gorgeous. I mean, hats off to Miss Barker—she must have been an absolute legend. I have a lot to live up to there. Sustainable vegetable garden (grey water only)—check! Sustainable chickens in charming coop constructed from recycled locally sourced timber— check! Mural depicting Snowy Mountains Hydro-Electric Scheme, designed by the children themselves—check! Self-published book *Tommy the Talbingo Turtle*, starring classroom pet turtle—check! Three-foot-high maze (once again I'm reminded of *The Shining*) planted by Miss Barker and the kids three years ago—I mean, what kind of dementedly zealous teacher plants a *maze*? And for what possible fucking purpose? Even as they were showing me around, one of the littlies got lost in it and started howling and it took me twenty solid minutes to calm her down. No—thank *you*, Miss Barker!

The school itself has one large classroom, a small yet well-stocked library, an indoor games room for rainy days and an office in which Glenda lurks, like a large, dumpy passive–aggressive spider (*stop it!*). The classroom is festooned with the children's artwork and lovingly hand-crafted posters: Save our planet; Our daily routine; Be happy, be bright, be YOU! And *labels*! She's labelled everything that couldn't get up and run away from her, as far as I can see: *door, chair, pot plant, fish tank, electric sharpener.* All carefully inscribed in blue texta in her nice round hand, then laminated. She's an absolute fiend with the laminator.

Seriously, she's clearly one of those 'Teaching Is My Life, and The Children Are Everything To Me' kind of teachers, and I didn't mean that to sound as mean-spirited as it came out. She's just super dedicated. And obviously the kids are very bonded to her and are not coping brilliantly with her departure. They're a bit shy, a bit stand-offish, but I guess that's understandable given they've only ever had Miss Barker in their lives, and whatever has gone down, it's happened pretty suddenly and unexpectedly. So I guess I just need to give it time. Meanwhile, I'm being super fun and super nice! Like this morning I spent all this time chatting and playing games, and letting them show me around the school, and we did 'Fun Facts' and 'Find A Word' and read the bum jokes book, which usually always goes down a treat but they didn't actually laugh that much, and then this little girl (Brody) put up her hand, and I say, 'Yes, Brody?' and she says, 'When is Miss Barker coming back?'

Never, I hope, because I want this job.

I didn't actually say that. But I thought it. And it was a bit awkward, because it seems like the children might be under the impression that she's coming back soon. I don't think anyone's explained anything to them. Because when the guy from the Department rang me up, it wasn't like, 'Oh, can you fill in for a month or two?' I was definitely given the impression that this gig was permanent.

So after school, I tackle Glenda on the subject—carefully, of course, because I'm fully expecting the waterworks. I say, 'Glenda, I don't mean to pry, but could you tell me what's the story with Miss Barker? It's only that the children are asking me when she'll be back, and I don't know what to say.' And sure enough, the waterworks commence immediately. 'We don't know, that's the trouble! We don't know what's happened to her! She just vanished! Up and left in the middle of the night!' And I'm like patting her on the sleeve and mumbling about how sorry I am. And she says, 'We miss her terribly! She was just the most *inspirational* person!' And then she goes on about how Miss Barker used to suffer with her period pains. 'I'd tell her, stay in bed! Take the day off!' And she'd say to me, 'I can't do that, Glenny, I can't let the children down.'

To which I'm thinking: big deal. Doesn't take a day off when she gets her period. Her and seventy billion other women. Still, I nod sympathetically, and Glenda takes a deep shaky breath and pulls herself together, and then she turns to me, and says brightly, 'But enough of that—what about you? How can I support you? What do you need? Just tell me!'

So I ask her about the wi-fi situation, because I've noticed there's no wi-fi in the house, and sure enough, although the school boasts several computers, one exclusively for my own use, THERE'S NO WI-FI AT THE SCHOOL EITHER!! They're on some antiquated dial-up system, which Glenda considers perfectly adequate. Apparently, rather than usher the children of Talbingo into the twenty-first century by updating their communications, Miss Barker elected to spend the entire Schools Bonus on a sustainable watering system for the veggie garden—I kid you not.

So then I ask Glenda about phone reception, because I don't seem to have any bars at all on my phone. And she gets all bewildered, and says, 'No phone reception?' because she thinks I mean the landline. And when I say mobile reception, she gets all short with me. Apparently, there is no mobile reception in Talbingo, nor will there ever be BECAUSE LANDLINES WORK PERFECTLY FINE. By this point, I am in absolute disbelief, and I say straight up, 'You've got to be kidding me.' I suddenly feel like I'm in a reality show where they withdraw all electronic privileges and see how long before you crack. And she gets all shrill and she's saying, 'What difference does it make? You have a perfectly decent landline! A phone is a phone is a phone!' And I say, 'Yes, but all my friends only contact me on my mobile!' and she shrieks, 'Well, I don't know what kind of friends they can be if they're that fussy!'

To which I think, Well, yes, point taken, they are not the greatest friends in the world but they're all I have currently. And then she says, 'If you're really that desperate, there's a spot up on the Ridge where you can sometimes get reception.' And I say, 'Where is this Ridge? Can I walk there?' And she says, 'Oh God, no, you'll have to drive—that's what I mean, you'd have to be desperate.'

Not wishing to sound paranoid, but I really get the feeling she doesn't like me.

Anyway, we calm down and we chat about other things, and I tell her how much I enjoyed the chicken casserole and that seems to please her, so by the end of it we're quite civil with each other. And then I come home and I get in the car and I drive straight up to the Ridge.

The Ridge is this spot high up overlooking the Reservoir, where, judging by the amount of empty vodka cruisers lying about, Talbingo's teenagers (not that I've seen any) go to party, or maybe just go to try to make contact with the outside world. It's a little bit eerie because the sun is getting low by now, and it's very deserted and some strange bird is making these odd cries that spook the bejesus out of me. I take a few steps towards the edge and I peer over. And I think, *Fuck, it's a long way down*, because way, way below, there's the water. Why isn't there some kind of railing? What stops those drunken teenagers from plummeting over? But anyway, I find a nice rock and I sit down and I look at my phone and, seriously, there is a tiny bar or two of reception wavering away. It's a very dicey thing, and it seems to entirely depend on a critical set of climatic conditions because it changes by the moment. So I sit there and I think, *Who am I going to call?*

And for a moment I feel this sudden intense rush of loneliness, because there is no one, no one I really want to talk to right now except Doc, and I can't very well call up Doc just because I'm lonely. I mean, he always says to call him if I need anything, but can I just ring him up because I'm sad?

I know I should call Mum and let her know I'm okay, but for some reason I just don't feel like talking to her, so I figure I'll call her tomorrow. And I think about Josh. Once upon a time I probably would have called Josh, but ever since he started going out with Delores or whatever the fuck her name is, things aren't the same between us. I get the distinct impression he is Establishing Boundaries with me, as per Delores's instructions. Quite often, especially after 8 pm, he just won't take my call anymore. Well, in the words of the great song, Josh: 'Fuck you, and uh, fuck her too.'

So then I think about my various girlfriends, and finally I call Sally because even though she really upset me with the Harry the Harelip debacle, she's still probably the one I like best. I mean, she's at least funny, some of the time anyway. And of course, it's not the same since the bub came along, and now she's had to go back to work to pay off the mortgage of their stupid big house, but I still feel like, underneath it all, she is actually there for me. Anyway, whatever, after several attempts, it finally connects: she doesn't answer and it goes through to voicemail.

So I leave a message, very jokey ha-ha about things, and tell her next time you'd better bloody well pick up, you stupid moll. Then I hang up, get the lonely rush again (tears pricking, manage to fight them back, take a few big breaths) and then I suddenly think, It's Friday evening! What the hell, I'm going to drink wine! And that thought suddenly cheers me up immensely. So I drive back into Talbingo and stop at the Talbingo General Store—which is licensed, fortunately— and buy myself a bottle of Jacob's Creek sav blanc and a packet of salt and vinegar chips. Which was dinner.

I'm suddenly buggered. Also drunk. Off to bed.

The weekend.

I can see how the weekends might be the challenge.

Granted, I wasn't feeling the best when I woke up. I really can't handle the wine since chemo, so I was queasy and I had a lousy headache. Luckily I still have a few anti-nausea tablets, so I force one of those down, then I stagger to the shop to get a Coke and some Panadol. That was breakfast. Then I lie down again. But I can't get back to sleep, and instead I find myself thinking about Miss Barker. How she would have slept in this same bed in this same bedroom. And I find myself wondering what the hell has happened to this woman. Why does a woman like that suddenly shoot through in the middle of the night? *Did* she shoot through? Or has something else happened to her? And given I live in same house, should I be worried? What's with all those locks on the doors, for instance?

Hours pass, the sun starts to come through the crack in the curtains at such an angle that it hits me straight in the eyeballs, so I finally get up. It's getting on for noon, so I have a shower, make some toast, and then I think, *What the fuck am I going to do with myself today?* And then I remember the bike. There's a shed out the back with some old skis and a kayak, and also quite a nice-looking bike. So I go and check it out, and it's got a few cobwebs on it and its tyres need some air, but I pump them up and it's fine.

By now, it's an absolutely glorious day. The sun is out, the air is fresh, the birds are singing in the trees. My headache is practically gone, so I decide to embrace the day and my new healthy lifestyle by taking the bike out for a spin. At first, I just doodle around the streets of the township, and I'm thinking: *Where the hell is everyone?* I ride past the park, and there's a few kids there with their parents, but I don't recognise them so I'm thinking they must be tourists passing through. Most of the houses look empty and have holiday rental signs out front. Once again, I am dumbfounded that they actually have a school here.

After about three minutes, I realise I've covered the entire town, so I get more ambitious and take the road leading down to the power station. It's a lovely gently undulating road, the Pondage on one side, the foothills on the other, a cow or a horse here and there. Little birds rising up out of the rushes on the edge of the road, making a funny sort of warbling sound. Looking up, I see a hang-glider wheeling. The sun feels so nice on my skin, and the rhythm of my tyres on the asphalt (a bit of a squeak now and then from the right pedal) is so kind of meditative that my spirits begin to rise and for a moment I feel exhilarated and joyful, and I realise it's been a long, long, long, long time since I felt like that.

Then ...

I come around a corner and there's a fucking 1960s sci-fi power station, like some kind of reinforced bunker where Dr Evil might live, surrounded by all these giant transmission towers and an enormous grid of powerlines crisscrossing the sky. I stop my bike, and I listen, and I swear to God these towers are emitting this ominous low-level humming sound. Even (did I imagine this?) the odd crackle. I don't like it. I suddenly remember all those stories about links between cancer and electrical transmissions. God only knows if there's any truth to them, but I sure as hell threw away my electric blanket, just to be on the safe side.

Anyway, I panic. Next thing I know, I've spun around and I'm pedalling away as fast as I can, and now the gently undulating road seems to be one long steep uphill gradient, and my right pedal starts slipping so that every time I put half a degree too much pressure on it, I almost end up catapulted over the handlebars. And just as I get back into town, I realise the back tyre is dead flat and, to judge by its mangled appearance, I have been riding the last ten minutes on the metal rim. For some reason, this just absolutely infuriates me so I pick up the bike and I hurl it into some bushes. And then I suddenly remember I'm the new teacher in town, and throwing a bike into bushes because a tyre is flat might indicate that impulse control is not my strong suit.

But of course, nobody actually saw me do it because the streets are completely empty and the citizenry of Talbingo is apparently skulking indoors, hunched over their Nintendos, despite the glorious autumnal day.

So I drag the bike out of the bushes in a manner that I hope might look nonchalant and wheel it up to the General Store, where I stock up on healthy provisions as best I can. I soon realise that they do not have a lot of what we think of as fresh food back in Sydney. In the refrigerated section, I find an iceberg lettuce, some apples and carrots, all a bit soft and limp and pre-bagged in plastic. Nothing is dated, so I have no idea how old anything is. Regardless, I purchase them all at top dollar. I also purchase a tin of corn kernels, a tin of sliced beetroot, a pack of Jatz crackers and some tasty cheese, plus a family-size block of Cadbury's Dairy Milk and a *New Weekly*. I look in the meat section, but it's too depressing for words. There are some chops but they look kind of grey, and some queasy-looking chicken Marylands that seem to be silently emanating E. coli even through their cling wrap. So I go to the freezer and pick up a McCain's frozen pizza (Hawaiian) and a box of hash browns. Also some ice-cream.

Obviously this can't continue. I am going to have to get organised and drive into Tumut to buy some decent food or I will end up with scurvy.

Meanwhile, the woman at the cash register has been watching me the whole time, and when I come up to the counter, she says, 'Aren't you the new teacher?' And I say, 'Yes,' feeling extremely embarrassed by my purchases (she also served me for last night's wine and chips—luckily not the breakfast Coke and Panadol; I think that was her husband). She introduces herself as Janelle, mother of the twins Jaden and Madison, and then says, 'Welcome, it's great to have you, thank you for coming at short notice etc. etc.,' And we get chatting about this and that, and she's banging on about Miss Barker and how wonderful she was and what a terrible shock it's been for the children and so on. I act all innocent and I say, 'Did Miss Barker get another posting somewhere else?' And she looks at me like she's shocked I don't know, and she repeats the 'vanished in the middle of the night' story. And I find myself saying, 'Isn't that a bit odd?' which of course I could never say to Glenda or she would probably sock me in the jaw. And Janelle nods and bulges her eyes a bit and says, 'Yes,' very quietly out the corner of her mouth because a couple of other customers have come into the shop. So I lower my voice also and say, 'Did the police get involved?' and she nods again and whispers, 'Missing Persons.' And that's as far as we get, because someone comes up wanting a carton of Winfield Blue.

I lug the bike and unhealthy comestibles back home, where I shove the bike back in the shed and spend the entire afternoon eating Dairy Milk and poring over pictures of celebrities without makeup in the *New Weekly*.

I should have been preparing class work for next week, but for some reason I just couldn't be bothered. So after I finish the Dairy Milk, I crack open the Jatz and the tasty cheese, then I finish off the remaining wine (about half a glass, sadly). I contemplate going back up the shop for more, but decide not to in case Janelle serves me again and thinks I'm an alcoholic. I try to watch TV (encore episode of *I'm a Celebrity . . . Get Me Out of Here!*) but the reception's not very good. I feel sick from all the Jatz and the chocolate.

Tomorrow, I'm going to start afresh. I'm going to get up early, go for a walk and then spend the day preparing class work. Also, must call Mum!

I've just spent about two hours on the phone bawling to Mum, and she's finally talked me down off the ledge. Her main point: I owe it to myself to hang in there and give it a proper go. And I know I should, so I will. But I am just feeling UNBELIEVABLY PISSED OFF.

Okay, so this is what happened. (I am actually finding this blog-writing quite therapeutic—maybe that's why they recommend it!) It's Sunday. I set my alarm for 6 am, but I slept through till about 7, then I rug up and go for a walk. And once again, Talbingo takes my breath away with its beauty. It's quite chilly, there's this silvery frost on the ground, and clouds of mist hovering on the Pondage so it looks almost mythical (King Arthur? Lady of the Lake? Must google, if I ever get the internet sorted). There's a mob of kangaroos grazing on the grass down near the water, and the boy kangaroos seem to be fighting one another all the time, grunting and boxing then having a little rest like it's time out, and then standing up and grunting and boxing again. I watch them for a while, and I think to myself perhaps I could start drawing. I would quite like to draw a kangaroo.

So I make a mental note to purchase a sketchbook when I go into Tumut.

I look up and there's a hang-glider above. This must be a popular place to hang-glide—possibly favourable air currents or something. Perhaps I could take up hang-gliding? That's exactly the sort of Bucket List stupidity that cancer survivors tend to partake in, Living Life To The Fullest etc. Am I living life to the fullest? Possibly not; possibly too much time spent staring at photos of celebrities without make-up. This is the whole problem with having cancer: everyone expects you to have mysteriously acquired some kind of wisdom out of the experience and, if you haven't, then it's a personal failing. I mean, people have actually said to me, 'Wow, I guess having cancer so young must have given you a whole new perspective on life?' And I always nod and try to look inscrutable, but in fact, if I am completely honest with myself, I have the same old skewed perspective I've always had, except now I get to feel guilty about it. Likewise, with living life more meaningfully. What the fuck does that mean anyway? How do you actually do it, in reality, besides taking up yoga? Like, I sometimes ask myself, How would I spend my last day on earth if I had a choice in the matter and was totally able-bodied? And invariably the answer always involves me ogling fish in some manner, either diving or snorkelling or whatever. I like fish. I like their pretty colours. I can follow them around for hours, to the point where I start to seriously creep them out. They try to shake me off by hiding under ledges, changing colour etc. One fish ducked into the wrong cave and got himself eaten by an octopus, which was the first time I realised that fish could look surprised. So all very educational, even fun, but is giving fish the heebie-jeebies in any way actually meaningful? I doubt it.

Anyway, I'm trudging along in the wet grass ruminating about all this when I come to a big sign explaining the Snowy Mountains Hydro-Electric Scheme. I spend some time studying it in the hope that I might be able to converse knowledgeably with the children on the subject. Apparently there is a lot of pumping water back and forth between the Pondage and the Reservoir via the power station, which generates electricity somehow. (How exactly? Must read up on this properly. Could be a good project for the older kids.) Three short bursts of the siren warn when large amounts of water are discharged into the Pondage. Unsafe for swimming or boating owing to the unpredictable rise and fall of water levels. (I guess the kids know all this, but it might be worth going over it with them anyway.)

Interesting facts: the original Talbingo is underwater; they flooded it for the Hydro-Electric Scheme. The Hydro-Electric Scheme provides electricity for 250,000 homes.

Anyway, as I'm reading all this, I start to become aware of this strange music. I can't figure out if it's bells or what, but it's playing some kind of clanging, discordant tune which

54

sounds oddly familiar but I can't put my finger on it. Then I realise it's coming from the church. So I decide to go and check it out, seeing as how it's Sunday morning.

My friends would probably sneer at this, but while I might be none the wiser for having had cancer, I do find myself a lot more open to the idea of God than I ever used to be. In fact, this is funny—since I always considered myself a non-believer—but I have prayed to God quite a bit in my desperation over the last two years, and sometimes it has really helped. Like, sometimes an odd feeling of calm has come over me. It's quite a pleasant feeling, and I realise I also connect it to my dad. Like, I feel as if my dad is with me and looking out for me, and he's been dead thirteen years now. Once, not long after I was diagnosed, I had this dream that he called me up from beyond the grave, and I said, 'Where are you, Dad?' and he said he was staying in a nice motel with tea-making facilities and a heated swimming pool, and I suddenly realised he was describing heaven. Dad was extremely unassuming; he never expected much or even wanted much, so I really believe that this was his way of telling me not to worry. That there was nothing to be afraid of, even if the worst happened, because they put you up in a nice motel. Which is funny, and it's very typical of my dad, and it's the sort of odd little joke that Dad and I would have together. So it was weirdly comforting. Of course, I never mentioned any of this to Mum.

But anyway, I wander up to the church. Here's another interesting fact: it is the first interdenominational church in Australia. Apparently, after they'd finished flooding the original Talbingo, the Snowy Mountains Hydro-Electric Authority agreed to build one new church in the new Talbingo, and by that they meant one church only. So apparently the different denominations had to agree to share it. Except there's no sign of any different denominations on the board out front—it just says in stick-on plastic letters: CHURCH SERVICE 9.30 A.M. SUNDAYS. FRIAR EUGENE HERNANDEZ. ALL WELLCOME.

It's quite a groovy sixties building, wrought from local stone, high up overlooking the Pondage. It probably has the best view in the whole town. Also, it boasts a carillon, which is like an organ except with bells instead of pipes, and that is what's producing this weird clanging discordant music. And here's the spooky bit: I suddenly recognise the song that's being played—it's 'Elenore', by the Turtles. I kid you not. So now I am totally thinking of my dad, because Dad used to sing that to me when I was little. (I wouldn't let him sing it to me when I was an angry teenager, of course, which is one of the billion things I regret bitterly now.)

I wander in. By this time, I guess, it's a bit after 8 o'clock. I assume the man hunched over the carillon must be Friar Eugene Hernandez, although he's not wearing robes or any-thing—just a black skivvy with a chunky cross medallion hanging around his neck. He's a funny-looking guy—very tall, very thin—and he's banging away at the pedal thingies, completely oblivious to me. The thought 'praying mantis' immediately comes into my mind—something about his long skinny arms. But then suddenly he looks up and sees me, and immediately he leaps up to say hello, and he's very friendly and talkative and starts blathering on about the carillon, and how he likes to play it nice and early every Sunday morning to remind everyone that there's a church service. And I say, 'Wasn't that "Elenore" you were just playing?' and he says, 'Yes!', really delighted that I actually recognised the tune, and then I tell him about how my dad used to sing that song to me when I was little. And as I'm saying this, I find myself choking up a bit. And Friar Hernandez pats me on the arm, very kind and sympathetic, and he says, 'Come and have a cup of tea.' Then he takes me into this little room at the side of the church.

Now here it starts to get strange. He doesn't make me a cup of tea at all—instead he rummages around at the bottom of a cupboard and pulls out this bottle of what looks like communion wine. And he says, 'Shall we?', and he has this gleeful look on his face like a naughty kid. And I say, 'Sure! Why not?', because for some reason it doesn't seem completely out of order to be guzzling red wine at 8 o'clock in the morning, it just seems kind of a fun idea. So he pours it into two big mugs, and it tastes actually rancid, but he says, 'Don't worry, it gets better about the third or fourth sip.' And weirdly, it does. And he's so nice and kind and interested in me that the next thing I know I'm blurting out my entire cancer story to him. The whole thing, right back to scratching my armpit and up to and including the fact that I haven't yet got around to getting the nipple done. Which is totally not like me, because I usually make it a point not to tell people about the breast cancer, and I certainly don't tell anyone that I haven't got a nipple. And here I am using the word 'nipple' over and over again in front of this crazy-looking, wine-guzzling Praying Mantis. And he just seems extremely understanding and sympathetic, and he keeps murmuring, 'Extraordinary. Extraordinary.' It's actually just a huge relief to talk to someone.

And then he says, 'Are you familiar with Psalm 38?' And I say, 'No.' And then he picks up this Bible, and he opens it up to this psalm, and hands it to me and says, 'Read it.' And as I read it, I start to get this churning feeling in my gut.

Oh Lord, do not rebuke me, I am feeble and broken. There is no soundness in my flesh, nor any health in my bones because of my sin. My wounds are foul and festering because of my foolishness. My loins are full of inflammation. My friends stand aloof from my plague, and my relatives stand far off. Do not forsake me, O Lord, do not be far from me, come quickly to help me etc. etc.

Seriously.

I mean, it went on and on and on, but that is the overall gist of it.

So I get to the end of this, and I'm thinking, *Fuck.*

And I look up at him, and he's just watching me, kind of like he's studying me. So I say, 'Why exactly did you want me to read this?'

And he says, 'Well, I'll tell you. You talk as though having cancer was just random bad luck, but that's actually not the case. Cancer is caused by a demon—or at least, the impetus which drives the cancer is demonic. And how does a demon enter the body? Through an open door. At the very least, you left the door open and it wandered in of its own accord but, more likely, you have unwittingly invited it.'

All this said in a very calm rational voice, like it's a perfectly reasonable statement.

And then he offers to exorcise my demon.

Again, seriously.

So I say, 'I think the demon's already been exorcised, don't you? Isn't that what a mastectomy is?' And he goes, 'No, that's just an excision. You're talking about the physical removal of a section of afflicted tissue. I'm talking about something more complex than that; I'm talking about *that which afflicts you*.'

And something about those words '*that which afflicts you*', out of nowhere, I start to cry. Tears just rolling down my cheeks. A great feeling of sadness, a kind of bottomless sadness. He takes hold of my hand now and he leans forward and says,

'Look, would you at least let me say a prayer for you?' And I say, 'You mean a prayer to get rid of my demons?' And he nods. And even though he's obviously completely insane and his lips have gone black from the wine, I think, *All right. Why not? What harm can it do? I'm probably rattling with them.*

Next thing I know, the Praying Mantis is standing over me and he rests his icy hand on my forehead and starts murmuring this prayer. And as he goes on, he gets louder and louder and starts pressing down harder on my forehead, forcing my head back. And he's reeling off every word for a bad thing he can think of. *'All demons, all devils, all pets of the devil, all incubi, succubi, all fallen angels that prey upon mortal women, wishing to plant their seed, all unclean spirits, demon missives, serpents and scorpions, and all those demons that afflict the body and stimulate cell mutation and cancer growth'*—I am not kidding, the list went on and on, these are just the ones that I remember. And now he's really starting to hurt my neck because he is pushing my head back so hard and he's shouting, *'I command you to leave, in the name of Jesus Christ and the Holy Spirit!'*

And now I'm suddenly feeling like I'm going to throw up. I open my eyes, and he's holding this fucking great crucifix over me, and shouting at the top of his lungs, *'Out! Out! Be gone!'*

With all the strength I can muster, I push him away from me and I just get the fuck out of there as fast as I can.

And I basically run all the way back to this house, and I bolt all those door locks. Front and back. All of them. I am so angry, I am literally shaking; I am literally vibrating with rage. How dare he? How fucking dare he? And I think, *I've got to get out of here. I can't stay. I don't like this place, I don't like this place at all.* And I pull out my suitcase and I start throwing clothes in it. But my guts are still really churning and I'm feeling really sick, so I go to the toilet and stick my fingers down my throat, and all I achieve is throwing up the rancid red wine and I'm pretty sure the Tamoxifen I took this morning as well. And then in the middle of all that, Mum calls on the landline. So she cops the lot. I don't even tone down the swearing.

At the very least, you left the door open and it wandered in of its own accord but, more likely, you have unwittingly invited it.

How exactly did I invite it? By wearing underwire bras occasionally? Go fuck yourself, Friar Hernandez.

Oh, and this other really weird thing happens. I forgot to tell Mum this bit, but it's actually kind of funny. When I run out of the church and onto the street, I suddenly realise someone is hurrying after me, calling out to me. Not Friar Hernandez, but this funny little sparrow-like woman who's been standing in the vestibule counting hymn books; I almost plough into her in my desperation to get out of there. She's scurrying after me now, going, 'Excuse me! Excuse me!' So I swing around and very rudely, because I'm so fucking furious, I go, 'WHAT?'

And she hands me this leaflet about a decoupage workshop.

No, first she literally cowers away from me like she's terrified I'm going to hit her, and then she plucks up her courage and hands me the leaflet about the decoupage workshop.

Of course, I'm very apologetic when I see her cower, because this woman is so tiny and birdlike it's almost like she might have some strange bone condition or something. She's probably about fifty, though it's hard to tell, and she's all dressed up in her Sunday suit, including MATCHING HAT AND GLOVES! What year is this??? Have I been catapulted back to 1950??? And everything seems slightly too big for her, like she's shrunk. Her manner is very nervous and tremulous, and she speaks very rapidly and breathlessly as if it's a matter of great urgency, and she says, 'I just wanted to say, you need to keep yourself busy here. Keep yourself active, in mind and in body. Do you have any hobbies?'

Hobbies, for Christ's sake. She wants to talk about hobbies. And even though this is the last thing I want to be chatting about straight after I've had my demons exorcised, I think for a moment, and I realise, Shit, I actually don't have any hobbies. So I say, 'Reading,' which is pretty lame, considering I spent about three hours yesterday flicking through one issue of *New Weekly*, which I hardly think could be described as reading.

But Little Sparrow says, 'No, not reading. We discourage reading. No, you need tasks—simple, pleasurable tasks—to keep your mind occupied. I saw you bicycling yesterday—that's an excellent activity. Long brisk walks, nine holes of golf. Anything really, just as long as it doesn't tire the lungs or heat the blood excessively. The Women's Auxiliary run craft workshops once a month. This month it's decoupage—will you come?'

And I say, 'Well, look, I might—I'll see how I go. I'm not much of a craft person.'

And then she gets very serious, and she leans in and I get a whiff of eau de cologne, and mothballs, not entirely unpleasant. She says, 'I can see you think I'm being intrusive. I don't mean to bother you, it's just that the isolation can be so difficult. The feeling that the mountains are pressing in upon you. I worry especially for the younger people, like yourself

------

Okay I'm back. I dropped the story there, because I suddenly came over incredibly sleepy and had to go and lie down, and then I slept for a solid three hours.

When I woke, it was getting dark outside. So I got up and I put a coat on and went for a walk, and suddenly I felt better about everything. Talbingo looked so beautiful with the sun low in the sky, and the air felt so fresh and cool that breathing it was like drinking from a mountain stream. I climbed up to the back of the golf course near the pine trees, and met a couple of friendly old horses who ambled over to say hello. I like horses. Tomorrow I'll bring them some apples. Then on the way back, I saw a few of the kids from school tearing around the golf course on their bikes, and they called out to me, 'Miss! Miss!' and they were really excited to see me, and we chatted about this and that. So that was really nice. And the kangaroos were coming down from the hills to graze near the Pondage, and I could see a couple of them had joeys hanging out of their pouches. And then I came home and I cooked myself a stir-fry, and I thought, *Okay. I can do this. Stay away from the Praying Mantis and everything will be all right.*

I've had a pretty good week so far. Which just goes to show how important attitude is. Working hard to be positive, instead of defaulting to my usual 'woe is me the world is fucked and I am the only sane one' position. Even Glenda's been okay for the most part.

The kids and I are still in the 'getting to know you' stage, but mostly I have to say it's going pretty well. There have been a couple of minor bust-ups. The younger girls in particular find it hard to adapt to different teaching styles. Yesterday Brody burst into tears when I failed to give her an *Awesome!!* sticker on her spelling test. Apparently Miss Barker had some elaborate marking system which involved awarding stickers saying things like *Awesome!!*, *Wow!!* and *Keep it up!!* in various confusing combinations depending on the mark. Clearly she must have had shares in a Taiwanese sticker empire, because Brody directs me to the sticker cupboard, which is literally chock-full of stickers, each with about a gazillion exclamation marks. Then she explains Miss Barker's ludicrous overcomplicated sticker-awarding system to me in exhaustive detail until my eyes glaze over and my head explodes.

Finally I say, 'Gee, that's great, Brody, but guess what? My method is different. Here's what I do: I draw a smiley face.' That's right, a hastily scribbled red-biro smiley face, which I think should be sufficient. I dug in on this: I wasn't going to give ground. Suck it up, Brody: new teacher, new methods. Far be it from me to criticise Miss Barker, but in my humble opinion, stickers are a slippery slope. Kids get all demented and competitive about them. Case in point: Brody. Sheesh.

Anyway, we got through it eventually. But to be honest, it felt good not to be pussyfooting around the ghost of Miss Barker the Absconder. I think the kids respected me for it. I'm thinking I might shake up the seating arrangement too. At the moment, it's all very uniform, everyone organised in their year groups. But sometimes it's good to mix it up a bit, keep it fresh. Maybe I'll work on that tonight.

The other slight fly in the ointment is Ryan. He is the oldest of the kids and is supposed to be twelve, although he looks seriously fourteen and appears to have bumfluff, so is obviously in the throes of some sort of early-onset pubescence. He's a lump of a kid, and quite frankly he gives me the creeps. We were doing group reading on Tuesday and I asked him to read aloud. He refused point-blank, and then Lucy says, 'Miss Barker always does private reading with Ryan.' Because apparently he is too shy to read out loud in front of the class. One thing he is not shy about, however, is gawking at my breasts. I actually thought I must have had my shirt unbuttoned because every time I looked up, he was staring at my boobs. And then later on, when I was bending over Oliver's desk correcting his work, Ryan got up from his seat and brushed up right behind me like a sleazy old perve. Like totally rubbed up against me, pretending to get past. I straighten up like a shot, and say, 'What are you doing out of your seat, Ryan?' and he smirks and says, 'I'm just feeding Tommy, Miss.' And I'm like, 'You can get up and feed Tommy when I tell you to. Get back to your seat.' And then he slithers past me to get back to his seat. Eeek. Get this kid to high school.

But otherwise I think I'm making progress. I've organised an informal Parent–Teacher Night next week so I can talk to the parents and find out more about the kids blah blah. So that should be useful. Also, I'm walking a lot and eating pretty well.

Five Things I Can Be Grateful About Today:

1. I have a great job.
2. I am cancer-free.
3. Madison and Grace very shyly presented me with Silkie's egg today, and apparently Silkie hardly ever lays so it was extra-special! I practically choked up. Sweet kids.
4. I live in this nice little cottage, rent fully paid by the Education Department!
5. The Pritchett kids' mum said the kids thought I was 'cool'.

Also, I suddenly realised today that I haven't had any twinging for a long time. When did that stop??

The new seating arrangement did not go over so well. There were tears. Like actual inconsolable sobbing. Recriminations were hurled, mostly comparing me unfavourably to Miss Barker. Brody told me she hated me (feelings mutual there). There were phone calls from concerned parents. Glenda accused me of 'meddling for meddling's sake'. So after gritting my teeth and persevering for almost two days, this afternoon I cave and put everyone back where they used to be. Then, as soon as the bell went, I drove all the way into Tumut to buy a carton of wine, so Janelle won't tell everyone I'm an alcoholic. Drove back against the setting sun, narrowly avoiding a head-on collision, then cracked open a bottle and guzzled. Goodnight

----

Can't sleep.

Still no sleep. This is ridiculous.

This is why I shouldn't drink wine. When I finish this box, I'm giving up. Alternatively, I could pour the remaining eleven bottles down the sink right now. But that seems a bit drastic, not to say wasteful of money. That's like a $130 literally down the gurgler. Also, I practically got killed on the drive back from Tumut so the least I can do is drink the stuff. I mean, I could very well be dead right now.

What happened was I got stuck behind a bus.

I mean, let's face it, it's a hideous drive at the best of times. You've got the mountains on one side and the Tumut River on the other and it just twists and turns the entire way. Sure, it's spectacular, but what good is spectacular when you can't take your eyes off the road for literally one second? To add to my misery, the sun is going down, which means it's directly in my eyes the whole way and because my windscreen is so filthy, it's kind of flaring on the accumulated dust and practically blinding me. Also, because the sun's going down, all these kangaroos are coming down from the hills to the water, and for some strange reason, even though they are wild animals and thus you would think their survival instincts finely honed, they do not appear to notice the one and a half tonnes of smouldering metal bearing down on them at 100 kph. Or if they do eventually notice, rather than get the fuck out of the way, they figure their best option is to stand stock-still in the middle of the road—like that's achieving anything. (How are these guys not actually extinct??) So anyway I am dodging these nervous ninnies the whole way and, let me just say, it is not diminishing my stress levels any. In fact, the solitary good thing about rounding a corner and suddenly finding this dirty great bus in front of me is that at least the bus would hit any kangaroos before I did. Also, it blocks the sun.

Turns out it's the slowest, stinkiest, least roadworthy-looking bus I have ever had the misfortune to get stuck behind. It is creeping along at seriously 10 kph, yet this seems to require extraordinary amounts of fuel because it is belching out these vast clouds of diesel fumes. Obviously there is something very seriously mechanically wrong with it, because not only is it emitting all these toxic fumes, it is also making very unhealthy wheezy rattling grinding noises, like its innards are about to drop out on the highway at any moment. And my problem is that between Tumut and home there's no stretch long enough or straight enough to overtake it. So after twenty minutes of being stuck behind this behemoth, I start to get desperate. I feel like I'm asphyxiating, even with the windows up. I realise if I do not do something assertive, I will be stuck behind this bastard for at least another forty minutes and after the day I'd had, I'll be honest, I was hanging out to get home and inhale wine. So when the bus sticks its right-hand indicator on, I think to myself, Well, this must mean the bus is telling me that it's safe to overtake. To be honest, I'm a little confused about what it means. I'm thinking, Does this flashing orange light, dimly discernible through the road grime, mean 'Do not overtake under any circumstances'? Or does it mean, 'Here's your chance, sweetheart, go for it'? I'll admit I'm not fluent in bus semaphore. But I've hardly seen any traffic coming the other way so I decide to gird my loins and take my chances. And even though the bus is heading towards yet another blind corner, I pull out and start to overtake.

The minute I pull out, of course, I've got the sun back in my eyes and I literally cannot see. I slam the sun visor down, but that doesn't seem to help any because the sun is now so low it's below the actual level of the sun visor. So instead of reconsidering the whole thing and pulling back behind the bus, which is probably what I should have done, I put my foot to the floor in the hope I can accelerate my way out of this pickle. And immediately I'm reminded just how gutless the Corolla is, especially in a pinch, in a crisis, like when it matters. It's giving me nothing, and not only that but I'm suddenly noticing how long this stupid bus is—maybe all buses are this long and I've never actually realised. And I can't figure out why I don't seem to be gaining on it and then I realise that it's because the bus is actually SPEEDING UP.

WTF??? First it signals to overtake, then it speeds up to stop me passing!?! I can hear its engines whining right alongside me, like an aircraft straining for lift-off. So even though I'm absolutely flooring it, I find myself going around this bend neck and neck with the bus, except of course I am on the wrong side of the road. And suddenly I hear this ear-piercing musical horn blast and even though I'm blinded by the glare, I glimpse this vehicle, this mustard-coloured muscle car coming straight for me. *This is it*, I think, *I'm about to die to the tune of 'Dixie'.* I'll either plummet over the side of the road into the Tumut River or smash headlong into this hot rod—those are my two available options. So I scream out, '*God, please help me please please please!*' and miraculously—I do not use the word lightly—the Corolla somehow finds the guts to surge ahead of the bus. The moment I pass it, I veer right back in front of it, narrowly avoiding collision with muscle car.

Car goes past, another blast of 'Dixie'. Fair enough.

But unfortunately, what I've done now is I've cut the bus off. So it slams on its air brakes—this horrible gasping, wheezing sound, like something you'd hear in a respiratory ward—then its wheels lock and it goes into a skid. It's slewing and sliding all over the road, and I'm seeing all this in my rear-view mirror. I am literally whimpering. I am bleating like a lamb and just trying to get the hell out of its way because it is obviously completely out of control. And because we're on a downhill slope now, it's gaining momentum and it looks for all the world like it will career right over the top of me. So in my panic I slam the steering wheel hard left and swing the Corolla headfirst into a culvert on the mountain side of the road. Just in the nick of time because the bus hurtles right past me, blasting its horn.

Okay, I probably deserved the horn blast.

Then again, why the fuck did it signal me to overtake and then speed up when I started overtaking??

Unless of course that signal meant 'Do not overtake under any circumstances'.

Long story short, I spend twenty minutes mewing pitifully in the culvert before I dare venture out again. It actually takes that long for my hands to stop shaking. Also, I'm terrified that the bus is lurking around the next corner, waiting for me. Or worse still, I'll find it wheels up and sinking in the Tumut River. But anyway, after some difficulty trying to reverse my way out of the culvert (sorry, gearbox), I make my way very nervously, very trepidatiously, back to Talbingo. Thankfully no sign of bus (unless of course completely submerged in river, but surely I would have seen the skid marks??).

The minute I walk in my door, I crack open the carton of wine and guzzle an entire bottle. I don't even wait to chill it, that's how desperate

----

Well, I got to sleep, but I'm awake again. It's 3 am—3.09 to be precise.

I am just having the worst, most terrible dreams lately. Mostly about the cancer spreading, as usual. This one started with me flat on my back, being conveyed inch by inch into some kind of hulking great nuclear scanner, moulded out of white plastic like a giant scary kitchen appliance. (Which kitchen appliance am I thinking of? A slow cooker? A doughnut maker maybe?) They say, 'We hope you're not claustrophobic, but just in case you are, here's a buzzer to squeeze to get our attention.' And then they all scarper into another room like a bomb is about to go off. I just lie there, listening to the machine shuddering and clanking as it starts to come to life. And as I'm lying there, I'm thinking, There's a word for this machine. What is it? And suddenly in my dream the word comes to me: *remorseless*.

This brutal fucker will find everything, no matter how infinitesimal. Every last little tiny metastasis, hiding out in my brain or my liver or my lungs. I haven't got a hope.

75

And then I hear this voice, a male voice, eerily calm and kind of distant, telling me to breathe in, then out, then hold my breath. The machine starts banging and shuddering very loudly and violently. I'm thinking, Is that normal? It doesn't sound normal. And as I'm lying there holding my breath waiting for permission to breathe again, I suddenly realise that in fact I am not in an MRI machine, or whatever the fuck I thought it was, I am in James Cameron's deep-sea submarine, and not only that, but it has hit the bottom of the Mariana Trench, which is like twenty billion leagues under the sea! And now the voice is telling me very calmly and reasonably that the weight of all that water above means we are experiencing some difficulty ascending, and it is actually imperative that I hold my breath because if I don't, according to James Cameron, the deep-sea sub will literally implode. So now I'm starting to panic, because I feel like I'm going to pass out if I don't breathe soon, and I seriously don't want this submarine to implode and for it to all be my fault as usual. I'm squeezing my buzzer like a maniac but nobody's coming to help me. And the worst thing is, I realise (in my dream) that I have seen this exact same situation on James Cameron's *Deepsea Challenge 3D*, in which James Cameron had explained exactly what to do if you ever find yourself in this kind of life-and-death predicament at the bottom of the ocean, but I can't remember what advice he gave because I wasn't paying attention. In fact, at one point I took my 3D glasses off and had a little snooze. Which is my whole problem, according to James Cameron: I don't pay enough attention,

I never have, which is why I get myself into these terrible scenarios time and time again.

When I woke up, I had fingernail gouges on my palm from trying to squeeze the buzzer.

I'm sure it's the Tamoxifen causing these dreams. Though of course in this instance it could be all that wine on an empty stomach. Also, it's not helped by the fact that there are a lot of weird sounds in the country that I'm not used to. Like a lot of dogs barking tonight. And weird night-birds making these horrible lonely mournful cries.

So I lie in bed for a while listening to this cacophony, and then finally I get up and drink some Coke because I'm really dehydrated, and take about four Panadol for my headache. And, of course, I can't get back to sleep because I'm obsessing about Josh. He's the one who took me to see the James Cameron movie in the first place, and it's true that at one point I did take my 3D glasses off and have a little snooze, and I don't think Josh was very impressed by that because he is a science nut, also an underwater exploration nut. I actually met Josh on a dive boat on the Great Barrier Reef when we were paired up as dive buddies, and let me just say that initially I was extremely pleased about this pairing because I had already decided that Josh was the hottest guy on the boat. As a dive buddy, however, he left a lot to be desired. He literally just swam off with his GoPro and ignored me, which is fine except the whole point of the buddy system is safety, and at one point I did actually get my buoyancy vest snagged and had to break off a whole chunk of coral just to extricate myself. So I was a little annoyed with him. But then—and as long as I live and breathe, I will never forget this moment—when we were hanging out at the five-metre safety stop on our way back up to the boat, he suddenly turned to me and he pulled out his regulator. I'm thinking, What's this jerk doing now, for God's sake? And then he reached over, pulled out my regulator and kissed me full on the lips.

Oh my God. It was unbelievable. I still swoon when I think about it now. Bubbles everywhere, literally surrounding us. And it wasn't a short kiss by any means; he wasn't hurrying. If anything, he was taking his time. It was lingering and delicate and explorative and absolutely bar none the best kiss of my entire life. Unforgettable. The imminent likelihood of drowning only added to the thrill.

Can I just say, the fish were staring at us. Like, they were goggle-eyed. They'd never seen anything like it.

After that, there was no going back. It was all on between us, we were inseparable. But as far as diving safety went, this only made matters worse because Josh's unusual idea of courtship was to swim past me at speed and pull my mask off. Or worse—and this was perhaps the single most terrible thing he ever did, unforgivable really when I think about it—on the third day of the dive trip he actually turned off my air supply. As a joke. While I'm underwater, twenty-three metres down. Seriously, one minute I'm happily watching clown fish duck in and out of anemones, the next minute I'm sucking desperately on my regulator thinking I'm gonna die. I mean, he turned it back on again maybe ten seconds later (he disputes this, and claims it was two seconds later), but still ... Even now, I just have to glance at a poster of *Finding Nemo* and I practically want to vomit.

All of which should have given me fair warning ...

To be absolutely honest with myself though, to judge from how sad I'm feeling right now, I don't think I'm completely over Josh. I mean, I make him sound like a lunatic, but really I think he's just a bit of an odd guy, a bit on the spectrum maybe, whatever that means. He claims never to have had a serious girlfriend before me, and I think all that crazy stuff he was doing when we first started dating (turning off air supply etc.), well, honestly, I don't think he knew any better. He was genuinely surprised that I was upset—I remember him saying, 'But it was just a bit of horseplay!' I mean, he was mortified that he'd done it when he thought about it. And the truth is, maybe I actually encouraged it a bit—the horseplay, I mean. We were so nuts about each other in those early days, we were like a pair of overexcited puppies. We were just always egging each other on. Like, one of our favourite games when he moved in with me was to hide in wardrobes, broom cupboards etc. and leap out at each other when least expected. Josh was better at it than me; he has more patience—also he's more devious. One time he spent the whole day lurking in our wardrobe when I thought all along he was at work. He was even texting me photos, supposedly from work—the colossal photocopier jam he'd caused, his lunchtime chicken burger etc.—but actually he'd taken these photos the day before. And if I'd looked closely, there were small clues he'd left deliberately, like a newspaper with yesterday's date propped next to the chicken burger. Anyway, around 5 pm I innocently go to the wardrobe to get my jacket and *GOTCHA!* He springs out at me. Seriously, in our four and a half years together, he gave me about forty billion heart attacks.

I mean he was completely obsessed with me. It was almost exhausting how obsessed he was. Until he wasn't.

But then again, sometimes I wonder, was it ever really a proper relationship? You know, like adults have. Open and honest, give and take, there for you through the tough times—like Sally has with Brett. Because sometimes I suspected that maybe Josh just liked having an audience, specifically a compliant female audience with great tits. He could pontificate about things for hours, often things I had no hope of understanding or absolutely no interest in, like quantum physics or German U-boats or medieval musical instruments. It used to make me feel dumb because I had nothing intelligent to contribute to the discussion. I did a lot of smiling and nodding and saying things like, 'Wow.'

Does he ever think about me? Is he sad too sometimes that we didn't last?

Answer, if I'm honest with myself? Probably not. He has Delores. Delores plays the lute, so that's one thing she has over me already.

Sometimes, as a form of self-torture, I like to watch Delores play 'Greensleeves' on YouTube, wearing a mournful expression and some kind of medieval wench outfit. Then I scroll exhaustively through the comments to see if anyone has said anything mean about her. But no. Everyone thinks she's delightful, so talented, 'this makes me so happy' etc. etc. Maybe no such thing as trolling in medieval lute world? Although there's one comment in Russian that has about a billion exclamation marks and a winking face with the tongue sticking out. I need to Google Translate it.

How was it that I came to stumble across this YouTube clip? Sally found it. She is an A-grade sleuth when it comes to digging up dirt on ex-boyfriends, plus she never liked Josh in the first place. She sent me a link to the clip in the hope it would give me a laugh. But I wasn't laughing. I was too busy staring at Delores' dewy white cleavage, displayed to perfection in her medieval peasant blouse.

I mean, let's face it, Josh has always been a teensy bit deficient in the sensitivity-to-others department. Case in point: as soon as your ex-girlfriend gets her breast cut off, make sure you start going out with a girl with the biggest bounciest tits ever. Just to reinforce the point: *Yes, Eleanor, breasts are important to me. Hello, Delores of the double-D cups.*

So I rock up to school this morning very tired and headachey from my bad night, and I find the children crying and Glenda looking absolutely ashen. Because all the chickens are dead. Massacred. Just feathers, claws and a couple of random heads left. No wonder the dogs were carrying on last night.

And Glenda says to me in this accusatory tone, 'We've kept these chickens for over five years and we've never had the slightest bit of trouble.' And I immediately feel like she's suggesting that I am somehow responsible for the chicken slaughter. Possibly she believes that I was so enraged by the seating arrangement fiasco that I crept in by cover of darkness and hacked them to death myself. But I refuse to rise to the bait, so I say, 'Well, it's obviously a fox.' And she shouts, 'What fox? We don't have any foxes in Talbingo! Besides, where did it get in?' She's got a point, because there's no sign of any holes dug or any other form of entry. It's all very weird. And then Ryan picks up a dismembered chicken head (Silkie's poor little feathery head, actually) and starts chasing the girls with it. And they're screaming very shrilly, very ear-piercingly, which is not helping my headache. So I start yelling at him, 'Ryan! Stop it!', and he's completely ignoring me, so I run after him and grab him by the arm, and he spins around and rubs the horrible bloody chicken head into my chest. And then he grins at me.

I'm in shock. Absolute shock. And I'm thinking, *This is assault.* So I go very calm, very composed, very icy, and I say, 'Ryan, go and sit in Glenda's office. I am going to call your parents.' Whereupon all the kids scream at me like I'm a complete fucking idiot: 'HE DOESN'T HAVE ANY PARENTS! HIS PARENTS WERE KILLED IN A CAR CRASH!!' And Ryan slumps down and puts his head in his hands and starts to cry. And I'm thinking, Gee, Glenda, thanks for telling me this in advance. Don't you think it would have been useful for me to know that one of my pupils has been *tragically orphaned*???

But of course, I didn't dare say it because frankly the woman terrifies me.

I wonder if Ryan killed the chickens?

Probably.

Let's just say I wouldn't put it past him ...

So anyway, apparently Ryan is looked after by an older brother. But the older brother is often away for extended periods due to his work, leaving Ryan to basically fend for himself. I learned all this when Glenda was sponging chicken gore off my shirt in the kitchenette. So I say, 'Well, that doesn't sound like a very satisfactory arrangement if his brother is away half the time.'

And Glenda says, 'No, it's not ideal, and that's why Miss Barker used to have Ryan over a lot on weekends and take him on special outings, just to fill in the gaps, because of course she was terribly fond of him.' And I'm thinking, *Fond of Ryan!* She was a better woman than I'll ever be, that's for sure, if she could somehow summon up some affection for this doughy lump. And of course, we must make allowances for the doughy lump's behaviour because he's terribly upset since Miss Barker went AWOL and, sure enough, Glenda's lip is trembling and she's bawling again.

But I find myself feeling very impatient with Glenda's water-works, so I say, 'How old is Ryan anyway? He looks at least fourteen.' And then Glenda goes a bit sheepish and says, 'Well, of course, Miss Barker held him back.' And I'm like, '*What???*' And Glenda immediately gets her back up and says, 'Well, she felt he wasn't ready for high school, and frankly I agree with her. Physically, he's a big boy, but emotionally he's blah blah blah—' I don't let her finish. I'm up on my high horse imme-diately. 'That is the worst thing Miss Barker could have done,' I say. 'That boy was ready for high school three years ago. Here he is stuck in the classroom with all these babies!' And Glenda goes puce with rage and says, 'I will not have you talk about her like that!' And she flings her sponge down and storms out.

At lunchtime, I try to go online on the school computer to find out what the Education Department protocols are when an orphaned student who should be in high school goes at his teacher with a disembodied chicken head. The computer is so infuriatingly slow to load that I give up. I type a note for Ryan's brother, asking him to arrange an appointment to come and see me at his earliest convenience so we can discuss in detail Ryan's multiple 'issues'. Of course, the printer won't work so I need to ask Glenda to help, which she does very sulkily with a lot of ill-tempered huffing and puffing. This is bad. I need to somehow repair the situation, because obviously this can't go on. Even though I blame Glenda entirely. God knows I have really, really tried with her. Mother Teresa herself would not be able to fill Miss Barker's shoes, in Glenda's estimation.

After school, I ask Ryan to stay back for a few minutes, and I attempt to have a little talk to him. I say, 'Ryan, I'm very sorry I didn't know about your parents. But what you did to my blouse today with Silkie's gory little chicken head was not good. I need you to give this note to your brother so he can come and see me asap.' And of course Ryan is staring at my breasts as usual and doesn't answer, so I repeat the whole thing and he finally lifts his gaze from my breasts and says, very sullen, 'My brother's away, Miss.' And I say, 'Well, that's not very good, is it? When is your brother going to be back?' And he just shrugs, like he has no idea. And then something really strange happens.

This mustard-coloured Valiant Charger with black tinted windows suddenly screeches up outside and sits throbbing and lurching at the kerb. Ryan's whole demeanour instantly changes. He looks out at the Charger, and he's no longer a big doughy lump of a kid but all sort of nervous and highly charged and alert. And he says, 'That's my brother, Miss. I got to go,' and I detect a note of panic in his voice. So I begin to say, 'Well, I would like very much to talk to your bro—' but before I can finish, there's an ear-splittingly loud blast of 'Dixie', courtesy of the Charger's air horns. Seriously. As if this is *The Dukes of Hazzard* or something. And suddenly I realise: this is the car I almost ploughed into when I was overtaking the bus!

Meanwhile Ryan's getting all agitated, and he's saying, 'I got to go, Miss.' And for some reason, even though I know I should seize this opportunity and go out and talk to Ryan's brother, I suddenly really, really, really don't want to. So I say, 'Okay, Ryan, well, just make sure you give your brother the note,' and he flies out of there like a bat out of hell. He jumps into the Charger, which then proceeds to execute this huge screeching three-point turn, at one point actually mounting the kerb and gouging up the grass, before roaring off in a cloud of blue smoke.

All this in a school zone, for Christ's sake.

I am so stunned, I just stand there for a solid minute, hearing my breath go in and out of my chest. For some reason,

I feel really shaken up. I go to find Glenda in her office. I'm thinking maybe this could be a bonding moment, discussing Ryan's maniacal petrol-head brother. We could get all indignant together. Possibly even have a laugh about it, like a team-building exercise. But the office is locked—she's already gone for the weekend, without even bothering to say goodbye.

Okay, so, fascinating new developments ...

Saturday morning. Managed not to drink too much last night. I get up at a reasonable hour, look out the window and it's drizzling, so instead of going for a walk I get my yoga mat out and start to do a few salutes to the sun etc. My plan was forty-five minutes yoga, twenty minutes meditation, then get stuck into preparations for Parent–Teacher Night next week. But while I'm downward dogging it, there's a low furtive knock on the door.

Almost—hard to describe—like someone is casing the place. Not expecting anyone to be home, but just surreptitiously checking it out.

So I think, *Who the fuck is this?* And I'm so grateful for the excitement of a visitor, that I spring up from my yoga mat and throw open the door.

And there, ladies and gentlemen, is the most beautiful man I have ever seen in my entire life. I mean, this creature is so jaw-droppingly ravishing it's actually hard to look at him, like it's hard to look directly at the sun. And I seem to have caught him by surprise because he's creeping around near the windows like he was just about to try my window locks. So he spins around and goes, 'Hi!'

And I say, 'Hi.'

It's a bit awkward, like I've somehow sprung him mid-nefarious deed, so he says, 'I'm sorry, I wasn't sure if anyone was home.'

'I'm home,' I say brightly. 'What—were you casing the place?'

And he laughs then. Incredible dazzling smile. Runs a hand through his tousled curls. Looks kind of embarrassed in an unbelievably adorable, incredibly handsome way.

'Oh, God,' he says. 'No, I wasn't casing the place!' And he looks down at this note he has in his hands. 'I just wasn't sure if I had the right place. Are you, like, the teacher?'

And I suddenly realise that this Greek god standing before me must be, in actuality, *Ryan's brother*!

Pause a moment to silently marvel how this can possibly be.

'Yes, I'm the teacher,' I say eventually.

'Wow,' he murmurs, gazing at me through the dark lashes of his deep-blue eyes. 'Incredible. Why didn't they have teachers that look like you in my day? Maybe I would have turned up to school a bit more often.'

And immediately I commence to blush and simper. Truly. I am so unused to compliments that I behave like this, even when said compliments are obviously completely concocted and laid on with proverbial trowel.

'I know this is weird, seeing you on the weekend,' he says, 'but I travel all the time with work, so ...'

'That's fine!' I cry out somewhat too eagerly. 'Please come in.'

But now he seems suddenly a bit reluctant. He's like, 'How long is this going to take?' And I'm like, 'Well, I think we have a bit to talk about. There've been a few behavioural issues and so forth.'

And he nods very seriously and says, 'I'm just thinking, now that I've met you and you seem a hundred per cent straight up, no bullshit—I'm just thinking, maybe I need to give this a bit more time ...'

I'm like, *What?*

'It's just I have to take Ryan into Tumut right now for indoor rock climbing,' he says. 'So ... would postponing our chat to this evening be out of line?'

Are you kidding???!! This evening would be splendiferous to the max! I have a date with the most beautiful man on God's earth! (Okay, not exactly a date.) What did I do to deserve this? (Did I mention that because of the drizzle, his curls formed little damp tendrils on his temple and the nape of his neck?) Thank you, God. *Thank you, thank you, thank you!!!*

He didn't show.

Not that it was a date or anything, it was a school-related appointment with a primary caregiver, but I still feel exactly like I've been stood up.

Possibly because I spent the entire day preparing for it as if it were a date.

I washed my hair. I shaved my legs and my armpits. I waxed my lady bits, incurring only minor burns. I blow-dried my hair and then went at it with the GHD. I plucked my eyebrows, a task long overdue. I went up to Janelle's and shopped for canapé-style nibbles (not much there, obviously—came back with Jatz and tasty cheese and a hideous dip professing to be 'tzatziki' containing what appears to be particles of reconstituted gherkin). I applied quite a bit of make-up but tried to make it look 'natural', even 'dewy'. And then I waited.

It was tough, because I didn't want to have a drink before he rocked up in case it looked bad. In case it looked like his little brother's teacher had a raging alcohol dependency, for example.

Finally, at quarter to nine, I cracked open a bottle from my stash. And I got stuck into the Jatz and tasty cheese, even finally, in my desperation, the tzatziki.

Eventually, I must have fallen asleep on the couch. Which is where I awoke this morning, covered in Jatz crumbs, to the strains of the Praying Mantis banging away at the carillon.

'Elenore' again. What a creep.

I have a few flashes of memory returning intermittently. Like I swear, I swear, somehow at one point we were dancing to 'Let's Spend The Night Together'—the Bowie version. Did he have it on his phone or something? Where did the music come from? And so loud! The whole house was literally shaking with it. Fuck, what must the neighbours think?? And this most amazing, amazing kind of salsa we were doing—seriously, it was like something you'd see on *So You Think You Can Dance*. This dude is a shit-hot dancer. I mean, unbelievable— like a Latin dancer, maybe? That would account for why he wears his pants so high, also his shirt unbuttoned to practically the navel. But he totally, totally knows how to *lead*. At one point, we were up on the kitchen bench, and I swear, I'm pretty sure anyway, I had my legs wrapped around his waist and I was leaning right back with complete fucking abandon while he spun me round and round, and I was laughing hysterically, because amazingly, my head was just narrowly skimming the benchtop.

So that's one memory. And I remember bits of us having sex, which was just unbelievably thrilling and exciting and would pretty much have to be hands down THE BEST SEX I HAVE EVER HAD, BAR NONE, and may I just say that includes Josh. At one point—maybe when he came?—he bit down on my neck so hard it was like he was the fucking Lion King. And I know that bit is real because I have the bruise on my neck to prove it. Even the teeth marks.

I'm not sure, I am fairly sure, because it is coming to me in flashes, that at one point we were both stark naked on the golf course, and definitely, definitely we must have fucked there, because I remember looking up at the stars and thinking, *This is so perfect, this is so perfect, ohmygodohmygodOHMYGOD*

I really need to try to put all this down properly because the last twenty-four hours have been extremely bizarre to say the least. The only thing I can compare it to for thrills and spills is the Wild Mouse at Luna Park—the most terrifying and exhilarating experience of my life, except the only thing is I feel like I am the Wild Mouse carriage that crashed, the one that spun off the rails and into the crowd, the one they have on display when you're queueing for tickets in order to frighten the fucking bejesus out of you.

Okay, so ... this is what happened, as best as I can recall. Sunday afternoon, maybe around five o'clock, there's that odd little furtive knock again. And there he is on the doorstep, holding a bottle of wine. (I have this horrible feeling I drank all that wine. Because I don't think he drinks at all. Anyway, it was delicious.) And he is very, very apologetic for standing me up the previous night. He says, 'Can you believe what happened? Ryan drove the Charger into the Pondage. Fuck it, that's the last time I'm giving him a driving lesson.'

Which begs the question—what was he doing giving a backward kid like Ryan a driving lesson at all, let alone on a winding mountain road in a hotted-up Charger, for Christ's sake???

'I can't blame him completely,' continues Gregory (that's his name). 'Some idiot was trying to overtake a bus.'

My heart practically stops dead.

I'm thinking, Is he serious? Has he seen the Corolla parked in the driveway and put two and two together, and now he's having a shot at me about that incident the other day? But he's eyeing me very coolly, very normally, not giving anything away. 'You'd be surprised at the lead-foots we get around here,' he says. 'For what purpose? Is it worth being dead just to get there a few seconds earlier?'

He smiles at me then, and I get a flash of white teeth. Can I say? Simultaneously terrifying and extremely arousing.

'So is Ryan all right?' I ask.

'He'll be all right when he stops crying like a baby,' says Gregory.

For the first time ever, I feel a slight pang of sympathy for Ryan.

Anyway, I invite him in, and I say, Would you like some wine, which he declines, so I say, How about tea? But he refuses on account of me having no herbal tea. He also declines water, on account of the fact that the government puts fluoride in it in order to turn us all into passive, unquestioning zombies. (Apparently Gregory is some kind of wild faun who only drinks from mountain streams.) So he sits down very formally at the kitchen table and pontificates for half an hour on the fact that Ryan apparently confuses Gregory's disciplinary techniques with those of a prison guard at Guantanamo, and consequently is always crying and talking back, and once even tried to smother Gregory with a pillow while he slept. 'And I am the sweetest, most docile person in the world, until you cross me', says Gregory. 'Word of warning: don't even try it.' And I begin to think to myself, *Jesus, what is going on in that house? Is this something I need to report?*

You see, I remember all of this bit because I hadn't started drinking yet. But Gregory insists I open the bottle of wine he brought, so of course I do. And from here on, everything gets very hazy. For some reason, what memories I do actually retain of the evening all have this strange bluish tinge to them, like we're under a neon light or one of those zapper things that kills flies in fish-and-chip shops. I expect that's the brain damage, because almost certainly I blacked out. I mean, the whole night was WILD. Did he spike the wine or something? Also, what's weird is I had no hangover. I mean, I've felt a bit strange and wired all day, but no headache, nothing.

What did he think about my reconstituted breast?! Did he say anything? I can't remember. But anyway, it didn't seem to put him off. Not like Harry the Harelip, with his 'Whoa. Whoa'. I'm pretty sure Gregory and I did it *multiple times*. I mean, this guy is seriously UNBELIEVABLE.

So anyway, all that was fine and dandy. Sensational, in fact. But as is so often the way in my experience, everything went to shit in the morning.

Okay, so at some point in the proceedings, I must have passed out on the bed. And I wake up with a start because I've heard a door bang. It's Gregory letting the screen door bang on his way out. Dawn is just beginning to break. So I think, Where's he going at this hour? Is he going home to cook breakfast for poor neglected Ryan?

I peer out the bedroom window, which looks onto the golf course, and I see him. For some bizarre reason, even though it's absolutely freezing and there's frost on the ground, he's bare-chested and barefoot. And he's crouching over a little and moving very stealthily. Every step he is hovering his foot above the ground a bit before he places it down. And I'm thinking, *What the fuck is he doing??*

And then I realise he is STALKING THE KANGAROOS.

Absolutely *barking*, as my mum would say.

So I go back to bed for a bit, then I get up and make coffee and some toast, and suddenly he comes strolling in through the back door and he's got these bloody scratches all over his forearms. He goes directly to the sink without saying anything, and he washes the blood off and then he dries his arms on a clean tea towel. I say, all innocent, 'What happened to you?', like I hadn't just watched him creeping around after kangaroos, and he shrugs and says, 'Nothing.' Like making it plain that he doesn't wish to discuss it.

So I say, 'There's some coffee in the pot.' And he's like, 'I don't drink coffee.' And I say, 'Of course you don't, how stupid of me.' And he says, 'What's that supposed to mean?' And I'm back-pedalling a bit here, but I say, 'Well, I've just noticed that you're kind of puritanical about things.' And he snorts and says, 'That's funny. Especially coming from you.' And I'm like, *What?*

And then the fucker turns to me and says, 'You wonder why you got cancer? Look at you. You eat crap, you drink caffeine and alcohol. You're filled with bile and envy. It's all cause and effect, you know. Nothing happens to a person that they do not deserve.'

I was floored by this. Slammed on the ropes. I was gutted.

But all credit to me, I fought back. I got very icy, which is what I do when I'm really angry, and I said to him very coolly, 'For your information, *fuckwit*, there's a fifteen per cent increase in survival rates if you're a light to moderate drinker.'

And he makes this scornful little 'Pffft!' sound again, so now I'm really fucking angry and I tell him very calmly to get the fuck out.

And he says, 'You're asking me to leave?'

To which I respond, 'There's no asking—I'm telling you. Fuck off.'

So he saunters very casually to the back door. And then he stops and turns back and he's got this odd little smirking, questioning look on his face, like, *Are you sure about this?* I reiterate, 'Fuck off, arsehole.' And he duly fucks off, letting the screen door bang behind him.

I was a total mess all day. For one thing, I couldn't stop crying. I was late to school because of it. When I finally got here, I gave the kids some worksheets I found in a drawer and sat at my desk with my sunglasses on, pretending I had an eye infection. Madison comes up to me at one point and asks me if I want a heat pack. I'm like, What? And she says that she used to be Miss Barker's heat-pack monitor for when she had her period pains. And she opens this cupboard and it's chock-full of heat packs. I'm thinking, Really? Miss Barker is discussing her period pains with a six-year-old and getting her to warm heat packs in the microwave? Christ Almighty. So I say very pointedly, 'Thank you, Madison, I do not need a heat pack. Not now, not ever.'

The weirdest part was seeing Ryan. This made me stop in my tracks a bit. Does he know I've been cavorting all night with his brother? And if he doesn't exactly know, does he suspect anything? I mean, he would surely be aware that his brother came around to see me and didn't come home. But maybe not . . . He certainly didn't indicate that he knew anything, just seemed his plain old usual dopey uninterested self. Anyway, I decided, best plan of action: avoid the kid as much as possible.

At one point, he did look up and catch me staring at him from behind my sunglasses. I just find it so hard to believe they are brothers, I guess I was staring at him trying to see a resemblance. Anyway, he looked up and caught me staring at him, but I'm hoping that because of the sunglasses he may have thought I was staring at Oliver, who was sitting directly in front of him. So then I say very quickly, 'Oliver, will you please get on with your work.' Which confused Oliver, because in actual fact he had been working, and of course he gets all bewildered and upset and goes, 'But I am working!', so I just say very sternly, 'You know what I mean,' and leave it at that.

Then at lunchtime I'm in the bathroom splashing water on my face, trying to reduce the swollen eyes, and then I notice afresh the big fat purple bruise on my neck, complete with teeth marks, which I'd been inadvertently flaunting all morning in front of the children. Anyway, I smother it with foundation, which helps only slightly. (I wonder if Glenda saw it? I don't see how she could actually miss it. Obviously, this will confirm her low opinion of me. But since when is it a crime for a primary school teacher to have sex? Albeit sex that involves biting. Albeit sex that involves being bitten on the neck by the primary caregiver of one of your students.)

After lunch, the night's activities caught up with me, and I actually nodded off at my desk. Like, seriously this immense weariness overcame me, and I just slumped over the desk and fell sound asleep, till finally one of the twins came over and prodded me awake. How long was I out for? I think, I'm not sure, maybe forty-five minutes? Anyway, I leapt up and we did some movement exercises to music, basically in a bid to keep myself conscious till the bell went. Then, as the kids filed out, I found myself hovering hopefully in case the Charger made a return appearance. But then I remembered the Charger is at the bottom of the Pondage, courtesy of Ryan, so I came home. I think I was actually half expecting, half hoping Gregory might be here. Which is mad. Because of course he wasn't.

Although I can still sort of smell him. He had a particular smell, hard to define—a little earthy, a little piney, a subtle note of spearmint leaves crushed underfoot. I should know, because I picked up the bloodstained tea towel on which he'd dried his scratched arms and had a good old inhale. Like, practically buried my face in it. And then I thought, What the fuck am I doing?

I suppose because I actually really like him.

I do.

Every time I inhale the scent of him, my belly kind of flip-flops.

I haven't felt this way about anyone for a long time. Since Josh. Since the early days of Josh. Since Josh pulled my regulator out and pashed me underwater.

Admittedly this guy is a prick. And I still can't believe he actually said what he said. But—and this is very hard for me to put into words—this tiny little part of me agrees with him. I do deserve it. All the crap I've put into my body. All the crap I *continue* to put into my body, even after the wake-up call of all wake-up calls, namely cancer. And also the bile and envy. He totally nailed it. I *am* filled with bile and envy, and also I'm a total consequence-dodger. Meaning I can never accept the consequences of my actions. I will always blame something or somebody else. Never me. And finally someone called me on it.

Nothing happens to a person that they do not deserve.

I am totally wishing I didn't tell him to fuck off.

I suddenly felt this compulsion to run down to the Pondage
to see if there's any evidence of the Charger. No sign of it.
(Presumably it's submerged? Or I wonder if he'd already
organised to have it dragged out?) So then I turn all
Miss Marple and see if I can find any skid marks or tyre
tracks. Nothing. But the reeds around the Pondage are so
wiry and dense, it's possible they'd just spring straight up
again if a car drove over them. Either that or Gregory has
just been totally bullshitting me.

Anyway, it's getting dark, so I turn around to head back
when suddenly I almost trip over this dead kangaroo. Lying
there in the long grass. A big buck, by the looks of it. Its
mouth is open, baring its teeth, and its front paws are kind
of contorted in this strange position. It spooks the freaking
daylights out of me so I start running and I don't stop till
I get home, and then, for some reason, I bolt all the doors.

Another bad dream. Three o'clock in the morning, and I'm wide awake and dripping with sweat. I'm sure it's the Tamoxifen. I should call Doc. Actually it gives me an excuse to call Doc. Obviously not at three o'clock in the morning . . .

Funny, I'm having more memories coming back from my night with Gregory. At least, I'm pretty sure they're memories (meaning I don't think I dreamed them, although that whole night has a weird fragmenty dreamlike feel about it). Anyway, at some point, after fucking however many times and biting my neck and all the rest of it, somehow we got on to the subject of ovulation. Because he can somehow tell that I'm ovulating. And he says, 'My problem is, whenever a chick is ovulating, I can't help myself.'

And I'm like, 'Seriously?'

And then I'm like, 'How do you know I'm ovulating?'

Because of course I have no idea if I'm ovulating. I am very out of touch with my body. In fact, I'm even hazy about whether or not I actually can ovulate while taking Tamoxifen. But I suppose I can because I still occasionally get periods.

And he says, 'I can smell it.'

I'm like, 'Really?'

And he says. 'Of course. Ovulation has a musty smell, like a damp cupboard.' And I'm like, 'You're saying I smell like a damp cupboard?' And he screws up his nose a bit, and says, 'Actually, yours is buried under another smell, which is chemicals or formaldehyde or something.'

How's that for pillow talk?

I reckon what he means by 'chemicals or formaldehyde or something' is the Tamoxifen I am forced to take, supposedly for another three and a half years. I am so, so tempted to stop. I'm pretty sure they make me feel like shit. Not to mention the dreams.

Not long before the Harry the Harelip incident, I went over to visit Sally and the new bub. I hadn't seen her in a while, because I'd sort of become a bit of a recluse, very antisocial, thinking all my friends were against me, didn't understand about the cancer, woe is me etc. etc. Anyway, Sally has this little dog, a cavoodle or whatever they call them, cute little thing called Barney, and me and Barney have always got on like a house on fire. I've often minded Barney when Sally and Brett go on holidays, and

Barney likes me because I let him sleep on the bed, also on their stupid overpriced highly impractical cream woollen sofa, plus I feed him treats on demand around the clock 24/7. So, Sally greets me at the front door and Barney comes running up the hallway, all excited to see who the visitor is, and then he sees me, puts the brakes on, comes to a skidding stop on the polished floorboards, and then commences backing up and growling at me. Like this very threatening low growl, and the hackles on his back go up. And he's completely fucking deadly serious. And Sally's all embarrassed and trying to make light of it and saying how Barney's had his snout out of joint ever since the new baby came along, and she's saying, 'Come in, come in,' and now Barney starts barking at me! I'm laughing and trying to pretend it doesn't worry me, I even try to pat him, which was a mistake because he practically takes my arm off. Or tries to. Finally, Brett has to scoop him up and lock him in the garage for the duration of my visit. It was horrendous. Then to add insult to injury, I pick up the baby and it immediately turns bright red and starts howling. (What is that baby's name? Kai? Jai? Chai? Something like that.) Anyway, I went home and cried my eyes out.

But my point is, I reckon Barney was reacting to the chemicals. He could smell the chemicals and he didn't like it.

I just went and flushed all my remaining Tamoxifen down the toilet. It took me a while. Then I chucked all the Zoloft also, just for good measure. Goodnight.

Another curious thing I just remembered about Gregory is
he's a vacuum cleaner salesman! That's why he's on the road
all the time. I actually laughed when he told me because it
seemed such a funny, incongruous sort of job for a guy like
him. And he got all offended when I laughed, and he said,
'Actually, I'm a very good vacuum cleaner salesman. You
know what I'm best at?' And I'm like, 'No, what?' And he
said, 'Getting my foot in the door.'

Totally fucked up at work today.

For which I completely blame Ryan.

So this afternoon, I tried to prepare a bit for Parent–Teacher Night. I had the kids doing drawings of themselves, so their parents get to guess which is their kid. (Okay, a tired old favourite, but it usually works pretty well, particularly if there are more than eleven kids and four sets of parents in the class—not including Gregory, of course. Sigh.) Meanwhile, I was trying to get the slide show together, constructed from snaps I have been taking combined with fun captions and balloon quotes.

After a while, I look up and I notice that quite a few of the kids have gathered around Ryan's desk, and there seems to be a bit of snickering. So I get up and go over, and of course there's a huge panic among the kids, and it turns out that Ryan is drawing a picture of a naked lady.

A naked lady that looks suspiciously like me.

Blonde hair—check. Missing a nipple—check.

Now I'm not sure if I interrupted him before he got around to drawing another nipple. And quite possibly this is just a generic 'naked lady' and not meant to be me. But something about the horrible resemblance just gets to me, and I lose it. I absolutely lose it. I rip the picture out of his exercise book and, in the process, practically rip his book in half and all the other pages fall out, then I screw the picture up and toss it in the bin. And Ryan just sits there like a big lump, smirking at me, which only enrages me further.

Then Glenda comes in to find out what all the fuss is about. And I say, 'I'll tell you what the fuss is about: Ryan just drew a picture of me naked.' And she says, 'I find that hard to believe,' or something like that to indicate that clearly I had misread the situation. So I rummage around in the bin looking for the drawing but I can't find it and I'm half demented by now, so I tip the entire contents of the bin all over the floor and I'm on my hands and knees looking for it and finally I find it and I show her, and she says—she actually says this, I swear—'Well, I don't see any resemblance.' And Ryan goes, 'It's not you, Miss,' and I say, 'Who is it then?' and he says, 'Just a naked lady.' Then all the kids start giggling and I suddenly hear myself shrieking, 'SHUT THE FUCK UP, ALL OF YOU!!!'

Which was bad, admittedly.

Anyway, Glenda says to me, 'How about you take an early mark, Miss Mellett, and I'll mind the children till home-time.' And I notice that she's eyeing me very warily, like I'm a rogue bull elephant and she's an Indian villager. So I realise I've got to pull myself together fast, or she'll be calling up the Department first chance she gets and reporting me for misconduct.

So I say, 'No thank you, Glenda, that won't be necessary. I'm fine.'

And she says, 'I'm not actually asking you, I'm telling you: go home.'

To which I respond, 'And I'm telling you: I'm fine. Thank you. Now go back to your office.'

It's a stand-off. The kids fall silent, watching us. And Glenda says very quietly, 'Will you step outside with me a moment please, Miss Mellett?'

I shouldn't have stepped outside. Because stepping outside gave her the power. The minute I stepped outside, she tore strips. How shocked she was at my disgraceful behaviour. How never in their lives have the children been spoken to like that. How she had no choice but to make a full report to the Dept. How I have breached the Code of Professional Conduct, and disciplinary action must be taken.

And suddenly I have a brilliant flash and I say, 'Yes, Glenda, you're right. I had an unfortunate outburst, but this is a teachable moment. I will go back in and turn the whole thing into PEL—Positive Experiential Learning. I'll explain to Ryan why it's unacceptable to draw naked ladies in class. I'll explain why the drawing upset me. We'll talk about how our bodies are private places. I'll explain that, although I was upset, I had no right to use the F-word or to raise my voice in that fashion, and I will apologise. Then I'll ask the children if they've ever got really mad about something, and maybe behaved badly or behaved in a way they wish later that they hadn't. What can we learn from that? That's right, it's all part of being human.'

By the way, I just totally invented that PEL thing on the spot. I was pretty pleased with myself, because thinking on my feet is not my strong suit.

Anyway, Glenda listens to all this, very unimpressed, and then she says, 'Well, you can do all that if you like, but I'm still making the report.'

It seems Miss Barker never once told the kids to SHUT THE FUCK UP.

More's the pity.

Anyway, Glenda heads back to her office, and I go back into class. Suddenly I just feel very weary, and I can't be bothered turning the whole thing into Positive Experiential Learning, though I make a mental note to write a book on the theory and make ten million bucks and travel the world promoting it. In the meantime, I toy with the idea of asking the kids not to tell their folks about my shrieking the F-bomb at them. Decide against it as potentially even more damaging, especially since Glenda's almost certainly sure to blab. So my harm-minimisation plan is just to be extra, extra, *extra* nice till Parent–Teacher Night tomorrow evening. With any luck the kids will forget it ever happened. God knows they don't seem to retain much else.

Parent–Teacher Night in two hours and I have to pull out all stops. I have to totally out-Miss-Barker Miss Barker, an almost impossible challenge. This is my Action Plan:

- Huge WELCOME sign illustrated by kids.
- Interactive guessing games (how many M&Ms in jar etc.) as bonding exercise for parents and kids.
- Display of kids' drawings of themselves—parents have to guess which is their kid.
- Slideshow of kids engaged in various fun learning activities, set to 'Time Of Your Life' for maximum choke-up potential.
- Science Discovery Table. (Chuck a bunch of magnets, pendulums etc. on table and hope for best.)
- Brainstorming Board—*How Can I Get the Most Out of School?* Everyone to write a response in different-coloured markers. Snore.
- PowerPoint demonstration on subject of 'Teamwork!'. Education is a *collaboration* between teacher, student and parents!
- Individual portfolios for each child, showing recent

samples of their work, plus learning objectives and hoped-for outcomes blah blah.
- Cupcakes, baked by me.

So I'm just going to ice the cupcakes, have a shower and then get back to school. My guts are churning—I'm so nervous. Also, I'm really, really tired because I stayed up till 3 am trying to finish the stupid portfolios. I hope they bloody well appreciate all this.

Might permit myself small glass of wine while cake-decorating to ease nerves (have been very good and not had a drink in two nights).

I CAN'T BELIEVE THIS.

JOSH JUST CALLED. ON THE LANDLINE. GOT THE NUMBER FROM MUM.

HE WANTED TO TELL ME HIMSELF, SO I WOULDN'T HEAR IT FROM ANYONE ELSE. THREE FUCKING CHEERS FOR NICE GUY JOSH.

DELORES IS PREGNANT.

FIVE MONTHS.

NO, IT WASN'T EXACTLY PLANNED, HE SAID ... (WHAT DOES THAT MEAN??? IT MEANS IT <u>WAS</u> PLANNED).

OKAY, I KNOW WE BROKE UP ALMOST THREE YEARS AGO NOW, BUT PARDON ME FOR MENTIONING, JOSH, THAT THE REASON WHY WE BROKE UP IS BECAUSE YOU <u>SPECIFICALLY STATED YOU DID NOT WANT TO HAVE BABIES</u>. **EVER.** DID YOU NOT BANG ON ENDLESSLY ABOUT ZERO POPULATION GROWTH, APPARENTLY ESSENTIAL FOR HEALTH OF ECOSYSTEM?? WELL, ECOSYSTEM SAYS 'THANKS A FAT LOT.' AND PARDON ME FOR RAINING ON YOUR PARADE, BUT WEREN'T YOU GOING TO HAVE A <u>VASECTOMY</u>??? WHAT HAPPENED TO THAT???

YES, I KNOW LOTS OF THINGS CHANGE IN THREE YEARS—I JUST HAVE TO LOOK AT MYSELF NAKED IN THE MIRROR TO SEE THAT.

AND YES, I'M ANGRY! WHY WOULDN'T I BE ANGRY??? YOU COMPLETELY FUCKED ME OVER FOR DELORES! HOW DID YOU EXPECT ME TO REACT???

SHIT, I'M LATE. ALSO DRUNK. FUCKFUCKFUCK FUUUUUUCCCCCCCKKKKKKKKFU

Let us draw a veil over Parent–Teacher Night.

It did not go so well.

Selected highlights:

Arrived late, swollen eyes, had obviously been crying.

Could not get slideshow working, in spite of extensive dicking around with computer.

Forgot to cover up love bite—parents commented.

Kept getting kids' names wrong.

Oh, and then Gregory turned up.

So of course, we had sex again. In Glenda's office. On her desk, in fact. With the light on.

While Ryan waited in the corridor.

Pretty sure that's a sackable offence.

I mean, everyone had left by then, of course. And Ryan was playing on his Nintendo. But still.

I have totally got to get a grip on myself. What is wrong with me?

I can't get to sleep. Just feel totally wired.

Tossed and turned for two hours, gave up.

I've been attempting to make a list of some of the positive things from tonight. Like, some of the parents were very nice. No one mentioned the F-word incident, so maybe Glenda hasn't told anyone. The Farnsworth dad (Ron? Rob?) tried to help me get the slideshow going, but even he conceded that the school computer is shite. Most of the parents seemed pretty happy that I was planning to drag the school into the twenty-first century, technology-wise. Everyone said nice things about the portfolios I stayed up all night labouring over, but I definitely got the impression that Miss Barker did that sort of thing about a billion times better.

All parents, of course, still obsessing about Miss Barker and her sudden departure. Janelle from the shop seemed much keener to discuss Miss Barker's menstrual cycle than her daughter's academic progress. (Every time she used the expression 'menstrual cycle' I remembered how Sally always used to say, 'I'm so hungry, I could chew the wheel off a menstrual cycle.' I miss Sally sometimes.) Janelle seems especially au fait with Miss Barker's menstrual cycle, because of course Madison is heat-pack monitor and apparently reports back directly to Janelle. So Janelle says to me, 'I know for a fact that she had her period when she went missing. And I also know that, unusually for her because normally she was like clockwork every twenty-eight days, on this occasion she hadn't had her period in a good while.' And she's gazing at me very meaningfully while she says this, like I should somehow guess what she's getting at, but I'm just too addle-brained to catch on. So Janelle leans forward and whispers, *'It wouldn't surprise me if what she was having was a miscarriage.'*

Jesus! Finally got to sleep, only to be woken by three loud blasts of the siren—they must be releasing water from the Reservoir, or whatever the hell that sign said. Surely sirens not necessary in middle of the fucking night? Seriously, it's 3 am! Who is recreationally boating at this hour???

I have been lying here stressing about Gregory. Our Parent Teacher interview was excruciating. Gregory kept saying things like, 'So do you think it's acceptable that the boy can't do his multiplication tables past three times three?' And I'm saying, 'Well, obviously that's a serious concern, but I would be very happy to give Ryan some special one-on-one coaching after school or maybe even on weekends.' And Gregory's like, 'Well, how much is that going to cost me?' And I'm like, 'Oh, I would be happy to do it free of charge'—the whole time just obviously hoping that I will get to have more sex with Gregory if I spend weekends coaching his dopey brother. And then Gregory says, 'By the way, what's up with your eyes? How come they're all swollen? Did someone punch you?' And I'm like, 'Well, no, actually, I just had some bad news about my previous boyfriend Josh, who called to tell me his new girlfriend is pregnant, and the whole reason we broke up is because he was adamant he didn't want to have babies etc. etc.' And Gregory rolls his eyes and says, 'Boo hoo.'

Empathy apparently not his strong suit. And then he says very dismissively, 'If you're so desperate to be someone's baby mama, at least make sure he's not a dickhead.' So I'm just sitting there, a bit stunned. I cannot emphasise enough that this is not the way Parent–Teacher interviews normally proceed. And meanwhile, Ryan is poking around with these two cupcakes on his plate, and I'm wishing I had not been so stingy with the M&Ms because those cupcakes look exactly like two breasts, and then Ryan very pointedly and deliberately takes the pink M&M nipple off one cupcake, pops it in his mouth and smirks at me.

Uuugggghhhh.

Oh my god, the most hideous thought just occurred to me—I don't know why it didn't occur to me before. Did Gregory tell Ryan about my boob???? Is that how he was able to draw it so accurately? Is that why Ryan took the M&M off the cupcake????? FUCKKKKKKKKKKKK

Jesus Christ, there is so much to write, so much has happened in one single day. But I think it's very, very important that I write down all this shit, even though it is very late and I am extremely tired, because I swear writing all this down is the only thing that is keeping me from completely losing my sanity.

Where to begin? Okay, well, why not begin where I left off, with the sudden horrible realisation that quite likely Ryan's drawing of me was not an unfortunate coincidence, but very likely Gregory sat Ryan down and said, 'By the way, your teacher has one breast without an actual nipple, and I should know because I fucked her. Several times. And she was extremely willing, not to say desperate.'

I drive myself so demented with this horrible, horrible thought that I get up, get dressed, look up Ryan's address in my student information folder, and even though it is four-thirty in the morning and pitch-dark and freezing cold, I just go right around there. I have no idea what I think I am going to do.

124

So their house is this ordinary fibro cottage, pretty similar to every other house in Talbingo except maybe a little more rundown. And sure enough, there's the Charger sitting in the driveway, looking all muddy and bedraggled from its episode in the Pondage. I try peering in the Charger's windows, which is impossible because they're so heavily tinted, so I try the door and, guess what, it's unlocked. Very quietly, very stealthily, I open the passenger door and climb in, because I have now full on turned into a madwoman. And it all looks pretty tragic inside. There are puddles of dank, stale water in the footwells and duck poo on the seats and ribbon weed wrapped around the gearshift. And I suddenly have this crackpot idea that I should somehow get the air horns going and blast Gregory awake with an extended remix of 'Dixie'. Except I have no idea how to actually do this. And chances are the air horns may no longer work after their dunking.

I slide my hand down his sodden velour seat covers. For a moment, I allow myself to fantasise about being his girlfriend. I imagine us pumping the music up loud and roaring down the Snowy Mountains Highway. And unlike possible other girlfriends, I'd never admonish him for speeding or beg him to slow down—no, I'd just laugh recklessly, tossing my head back, with the windows down and the wind blowing my hair around. The thought of other girlfriends prompts me to rummage through the glove box in search of any evidence of predecessors, and then, all of a sudden, Gregory opens the door and slides into the driver's seat.

It's like he hasn't seen me, although I don't understand how this is possible because the interior light came on when he opened the door and there I was, plainly visible, rummaging away in his glove box. But if he's seen me, he pays me no attention. He puts the key in the ignition and takes a moment to check his appearance in the rear-view mirror. Runs a hand through his tousled curls. Picks his teeth with his pinky fingernail. Spends quite a long time picking his teeth actually, like he may have just felled and eaten a wildebeest. For the first time, I notice just how long and sharp his teeth are, hence the bruise I've been sporting on my neck. I smell his earthy, minty, wild-creature smell and marvel silently at his beauty.

He turns the key and the Charger roars into life like a baited bear. He jerks the gearstick into reverse, puts his foot to the floor and belts back out the driveway so fast my neck snaps. Then he executes a very aggressive, very testosterone-heavy three-point turn, and we roar down the road towards the highway.

I am quietly freaking out. I mean, he is going so fast, I can literally feel the G-forces wrapping my intestines around my spinal cord. I don't know what to do. I'm thinking, Does he know I'm here or does he not know I'm here? I figure either way, maybe I should ask him to slow down a bit, so I say, 'Gregory, do you mind—', whereupon he jumps right out of his skin like he's seen me for the first time, and slams the brakes on. The Charger skids off the road into the long grass, stopping just short of a second dunking in the Pondage.

'WHAT THE FUCK ARE YOU DOING?' he screams at me.

The sky is just beginning to lighten now—it's this very murky grey light, and the atmosphere is so thick with mist that I can't actually see any kangaroos, although I can hear them thumping away in fright. I can't even see the Pondage because the mist is completely covering it. I can just barely make out the shape of the sign forbidding recreational boating. It's truly so misty it's like we're sitting in a cloud, and I make an observation along these lines to Gregory, but he is having none of it.

'WHAT THE FUCK ARE YOU DOING IN MY CAR?' he screams, literally at top of lungs. 'ARE YOU FUCKING NUTS?'

If I had a dollar for every time someone's asked me that last question, especially Josh. Still, it hurts to hear it coming from Gregory, so I decide the best thing to do is to act completely calm and composed, completely *not* nuts. So in a very quiet, reasonable voice I try to tell him that the reason I am lurking in his car in the wee small hours is because I simply wanted to ask him a couple of questions, specifically regarding what Ryan knows or doesn't know about my missing nipple. But before I even finish explaining, he completely turns on me.

He says, 'You know what? I really don't have time for this shit. And you know what else? You have no moral compass, which I find repugnant. All the more so because of your responsibilities as a primary school teacher. Here you are, charged with instilling in our children the moral values that will carry them through a lifetime, and yet you have no compunctions about engaging in casual sex with a virtual stranger. While intoxicated. Your behaviour appals me. And clearly the problem is systemic because the other one was just as bad.'

I am stunned.

I am rendered speechless.

I feel exactly like I've been punched in the guts; it literally hurts to take a breath.

So then I do this very strange thing. I open the door of the Charger, and I get out. I take a few steps forward into the mist till I can feel the water beginning to slush around my ankles, and then I start to wade into the Pondage.

Okay, so I admit I have always been one for dramatic attention-seeking behaviour in a crisis. Ever since I was a kid. If I got in trouble or anything, I would hold my breath—and I am extremely good at holding my breath, I can actually do it till I pass out. It used to scare my parents half to death. Also, it used to drive Josh mad. And once when we went on a cruise to New Caledonia, and we'd had a few too many mojitos in the Starfish Lounge and inevitably started fighting, I climbed over the railing of this fucking great ocean liner and threatened to jump, which was a very dangerous, insane thing to do, because I was standing on a very slippery perch about one-inch-wide and with the slightest roll of the ship, I would have fallen hundreds of feet to certain death in the Pacific Ocean. Josh was furious, as were the Sea Princess security people who threatened to put me off in Noumea and make me fly home, but I cried so much they finally agreed to let me stay. So what I'm saying is, I guess I was engaging in this kind of typical Eleanor dramatic gesture by walking into the Pondage. I think my plan, if you could call it a plan, was to walk right in and then hold my breath underwater for a very long time, basically just to scare him so he'd feel really bad about what he'd just said to me.

So I'm wading in through the mist, and I'm suddenly remembering that the sirens went off last night, which means they released water from the Reservoir, which must be why it's so unbelievably frigging cold—it's so cold, the muscles in my calves seize up almost instantly with cramp. It's agony. I reach down to try to massage my cramping legs, and as I do, my hand brushes against something slimy lurking in the water, which for some reason, maybe the texture of it, makes me involuntarily recoil. And I look down, thinking, *What is that?* And right there in the misty dawn light, I see it.

It's a hand.

A human hand, just below the surface of the water. A human hand attached to an arm. Which is attached to a body. All quite decomposed, but definitely recognisable as human. And the hand is open, palm up, what's left of the fingers slightly curled, and the motion of the disturbed water makes it look like—I know this sounds crazy—but *almost like this hand is beckoning me in*. And because I have bumped it free of whatever it's been entangled in, the other hand rises up to the surface now too, and this hand is clutching a clump of long stalks. By which I mean a loose clump of stalks, like it's pulled them out of the ground, because they still have their roots attached. And then, horribly, the head rises up.

And I know, I just know instantaneously, that this is Miss Barker.

Well, I scream—I mean, the sound that comes out of my mouth is barely even human—and I scramble the fuck out of there just as fast as I can. And I'm like, 'Oh my God, it's Miss Barker!' And now Gregory gets out of the car too. 'Miss Barker?' he says. 'That's bullshit.' So very casual, very nonchalant, he wades in to have a look. And seeing her, he changes his tune completely. He cries out, 'Oh God. Oh God. Oh God. Oh God.' And then he throws up really violently, like practically projectile.

I mean, I am shocked, of course, at the sight of the body, but Gregory is completely beside himself. He keeps lurching around, groaning and throwing up and clutching his belly.

I mean, even though it is admittedly a very shocking and unsettling thing to see, his reaction seems a touch excessive. And meanwhile, I'm thinking, *What do I do, what do I do, I better do the right thing for once in my life, I better go get the police.* So while Gregory is staggering around and vomiting and carrying on, I start running off in the direction of the police station. And Gregory calls out, 'Where are you going?' So I yell back, 'I'm going to get the police!' And he goes, 'No! Wait! Come back!'

So now it starts to get really weird.

He wades back into the water and, right before my very eyes, he grabs the hand that's clutching the clump of stalks and he is trying to pull the stalks out of the hand. I'm like, *What are you doing???* But this dead hand has a ferocious grip and it's not letting go of these stalks, not for anything. And I'm screaming at him, 'You can't do that! That's evidence! You can't touch the body!' And he's struggling like crazy, grunting with the effort of trying to open up this hand and release the stalks, and suddenly there's this sickening almighty cracking sound, and the hand actually breaks off the arm and he screams like a girl, I kid you not, and flings the hand into the water.

'Oh God!' he cries, and he stands there gasping for a moment. Then, next thing, he suddenly dives under the water, and he remains below for a tremendously long time. I mean, I thought I could hold my breath, but this guy is like a free diver. Five solid minutes pass by and I'm starting to wonder if he's ever going to come up. And finally he does come up and he's all panicky. 'I can't find it, I can't find her stupid hand!'

And he dives under again, and this time he stays under for what feels like ten minutes. He stays under so long, I'm actually convinced he's drowned. I'm just standing there, whimpering and fretting and wondering what I should do, and finally I wade back in, which I really don't want to do because of Miss Barker, and I'm calling, 'Gregory! Gregory!' And suddenly I hear a rippling noise, and Gregory emerges from the water right next to me. He's dripping mud and slime and pondweed, and he's furious. The word 'apoplectic' comes to mind. He's all red-faced and crazy-looking and the veins in his neck are bulging out, presumably from holding his breath all that time. I'm like, 'Did you find it?'—very meekly, because he's scaring me—and he's like, 'No, I didn't fucking find it.' Then he strides out of the Pondage, gets back into the Charger, starts it up and just reverses the fuck out of there. It's actually almost comical because at first he doesn't realise that the passenger side is still open, and it's snagging and scraping among the long grass, so now he has to stop the car and try to pull it shut but he can't reach it from inside, so he has to get out of the car and walk around to the passenger side and slam the door, which he does very forcefully to make a point, because of course he blames me for leaving it open in the first place. Then he gets back in the Charger and drives off at speed towards the highway, with a big gurgly blast of 'Dixie' as a final fuck you. Leaving me standing in the Pondage with what remains of Miss Barker.

So that was my Thursday morning.

Well, no, actually; that was just the beginning of my Thursday morning.

I did not like being left alone with poor Miss Barker. She was not a pretty sight. And yet I felt uncomfortable about just abandoning her there.

'Give me one minute,' I say to her. 'I'll go get the cops.'

I run up to the police station, which is a good ten-minute run entirely uphill, so by the time I get there I am really puffed out and exhausted and I have a really bad stitch. The police station is this little one-room weatherboard shack, with a big sign that says POLICE and a very tall flagpole from which the Australian flag is drooping like it's depressed. It's still early and the building is locked—there's a cheery SORRY WE'RE CLOSED! sign on the door, like you'd expect to see in a milk bar. Regardless, I pound away on the front door for a solid five minutes. Then I hear this irritated voice call out, 'It's closed!', and I realise there's a dwelling behind the police shack, and this woman in ugg boots and a terry-towelling bathrobe has come out onto the verandah. So I'm like, 'I need the police!' And she goes back inside, and a minute later this big fat uniformed copper walks out with a mug of coffee.

And he's peering at me suspiciously from the verandah, like he doesn't appreciate being interrupted during breakfast.

I literally scream at him, 'Miss Barker is down in the Pondage!'

Now he starts to take an interest.

So Senior Sergeant Saunders drives us down to the Pondage with one hand on the steering wheel and the other balancing his coffee mug on his belly. By now, the sun is just beginning to poke over the mountains, and the mist has mostly lifted except for these sparse ghostly patches floating on the surface of the Pondage. The whole thing is feeling so surreal that I'm beginning to wonder if maybe I actually dreamed it. But sure enough, there is poor pathetic Miss Barker floating gloomily among the pondweed. And Senior Sergeant Saunders picks up a big long stick and pokes her with it, and says, 'That's her all right,' because poking a corpse with a stick is his idea of identifying the victim. And he immediately hypothesises that she has floated down from the Reservoir when they opened the sluice gates last night. And then he says, 'Most likely she jumped off the Ridge. That's where they generally like to do it. Well, it's a good hundred-foot drop, isn't it? Plus, you've got the freezing water.'

So we stand there a few minutes staring down at Miss Barker while he drinks his coffee, and finally he tosses the dregs in the water and tidily rinses his mug, like he's a boy scout. I'm staring at him, dumbfounded. I'm like, *'Haven't you ever heard of contaminating the crime scene??*' And he's like, 'Guess who's watched too much *CSI*?' And then he gets distracted by these two big kangaroos getting stuck into each other nearby, and he starts commentating the action like we're watching Manny Pacquiao and Floyd Mayweather Jr. Every now and then he glances over at me to see how I'm enjoying his humour, and finally I get fed up and I say, 'Are you actually going to do anything about this corpse we have here???'

'Calm down! Calm down! Wheels are in motion!' he says, although clearly no wheels are in motion. And he tells me he's going to go back to the station to call the Tumut boys in, unless I want to help him drag her in myself.

I totally can't stand this prick.

So he's about to jump in the car and head back to the police station and I'm like, 'You're seriously just going to leave the body unattended?' I cannot believe how unprofessional he is. And he's like, 'Well, you can stay here and mind her if you like, but I don't think she's going anywhere.' And I'm like, 'I have to get ready for school.' And he's like, 'Fair enough,' and as I'm walking away, he drives past me and yells out, 'Hey! Tell Dracula to stop biting your neck!'

So I go back home and get dressed, and try to cover up my love bite as best I can with concealer and foundation, and then I head off up to school. The children are all clustered at the back fence, staring down towards the Pondage—clearly word has got out already because they all seem very serious and preoccupied like they know full well it's their poor dead teacher down there. I can see that the Tumut police are now at the scene—a number of officers have waded in, someone is photographing the body, a couple of them are talking to Senior Sergeant Saunders. At one point, he gestures towards the school, and the other cops turn and stare up at us. I have this sudden irrational impulse to duck down so they don't see me, but I realise that will only make me look guilty, so instead I just turn away and pretend to be closely examining the mural of the Hydro-Electric Scheme till I think it's probably safe to look back again.

I realise they are about to drag the body out—no attempt to hide the grisly spectacle from onlookers—so I herd the kids inside quick smart. And, of course, I have nothing ready to teach them because I have spent most of the night prowling around stalking Gregory, so I decide that now is probably the time to stick on a DVD to distract them from what's going on in the Pondage. I find one labelled *Talbingo's Got Talent!*, which turns out to be a recording of the school talent show, and I realise that it must be pretty recent because all the kids look more or less the same age. They each have a turn singing or playing a musical instrument or doing little comic skits pretending to be newsreaders, the usual stuff, but the absolutely mesmerising thing is that every now and then you get a glimpse of Miss Barker as she dashes onstage to turn someone's sheet music or adjust a microphone or introduce the next student. Quite buxom, full-hipped. A bit staid and middle-aged in her dress sense. A penchant for floaty scarves, secured with a brooch (in this instance, a cat brooch). Really lovely with the kids. Very gentle, very patient, always encouraging. And as I watch her, I am gradually overcome with a vast, bottomless sense of deep personal shame. The stark contrast between us is so marked, how could I feel otherwise? She is absolutely wonderful. Teaching is truly her vocation. No wonder the children love her. No wonder they don't warm to me. Me and my never-ending personal dramas. My love bites and my hangovers. My screeching the f-bomb at them.

And suddenly I realise that the children are weeping. Just quietly weeping. Big tears rolling silently down their cheeks as they gaze up at the screen. Because of course their beloved, decent, good-hearted teacher is being dragged out of the Pondage even as we sit there.

How could I have been so insensitive?

So I jump up immediately and grab the remote and try to turn the DVD off. But it doesn't want to shut off, it just freeze-frames on a shot of Miss B smiling at the camera, which induces a fresh bout of weeping from the littlies. Then, as I hit more buttons, it begins fast-forwarding in fits and starts, and stopping and playing in random spots, always featuring Miss Barker, then fast-forwarding again. Meanwhile I'm pressing the stop button like a maniac, but nothing I do seems to make any difference. I just about fling the remote at the television screen. But instead I control myself and run up and crawl under the desk and pull the plug out.

I get up and I turn and look at the kids, all gazing up at me with their big wet eyes and their sad, sad faces, and I literally do not know what to say to them. So I say, 'Where's Ryan?' in a sharp voice, because I suddenly notice he's missing. And Camille says, 'He's outside, Miss.' I'm so relieved to have a reason to get away from all those judging little faces, I run outside like it's a matter of utmost importance that I find Ryan. And he's sitting on a seat, looking down towards the Pondage where the police are still congregated. And he's sobbing, absolutely sobbing his heart out.

Immediately, my whole attitude to Ryan does a complete unexpected one-eighty. Frankly I'd always found him borderline repulsive, but now I see how grief-stricken he is and my heart goes out to him. I sit down beside him and put my arms around him, and I gently rock him while he sobs into my breast. We sit like this for I don't know how long, with me stroking his hair and him sobbing these great hacking sobs. Poor kid, I think. No parents to look after him. Just Gregory—and let's face it, Gregory is not exactly the motherly type. No wonder Ryan became so attached to Miss Barker. She was probably the only person who was ever nice to him. 'Ryan,' I say, 'if you're feeling sad at any time, or if you're lonely this weekend, come and visit me.' And he looks up at me with these big fat glistening teardrops hanging off his eyelashes, and he says, 'Can we make cupcakes?' And I'm like, 'Sure we can make cupcakes, if that's what you'd like to do.' And this seems to cheer him up a bit and then the recess bell goes so I give him five bucks to buy himself some chips from the shop. I realise then that the whole front of my blouse is literally sodden with Ryan's tears. And this blouse goes see-through when it's wet, which is kind of embarrassing.

So I'm in the bathroom trying to dry my blouse with the hand dryer when Glenda materialises, all teary and resentful. She's like, 'The police are here, and they want to talk to you.' Very steely, very accusatory in her tone. Immediately I panic. I am absolutely not ready to talk to the cops. I'm like, 'I'm too busy, recess is about to finish.' And she's like, 'They don't care, they want to talk to you right now. They're waiting for you in my office.' And I'm like, Seriously, *your office*? That's embarrassing. Because that is where I had sex with Gregory the night before.

Glenda's office is really, really small. It's basically a cupboard. It's so small it's actually quite difficult to have sex in. Gregory is a very physical lover—he likes to try all sorts of positions, and he particularly likes to simultaneously gaze at himself in the mirror, and Glenda has a tiny little hand mirror which he found in one of her drawers and, I am not joking, he literally held that up at various angles so he could better observe how fantastic he looks while having sex. And because he had trouble getting a good angle on himself with this tiny mirror, he kept arranging me in various different positions—doggy-style on the desk, straddling the chair, up against the filing cabinet, down and dirty on the carpet with my head rammed at right angles against the bookshelf. I wouldn't say he was a considerate lover, because frankly it is all about Gregory. But in its own way it is quite exciting, especially if you don't mind a bit of carpet burn.

So here I am with my love bite and my see-through blouse, thinking about having sex with Gregory while simultaneously being interviewed by the police in the actual love den. I notice a bunch of incriminating tissues in the wastepaper bin, and a strand of my hair entangled in the metal handle of the filing cabinet. But of course, the cops are so hopeless they don't pick up on any of that, although I do wonder about Glenda. She'd notice, for sure. Plus, we did leave her desk in a bit of a mess.

Anyway, so I'm being interviewed in the love cupboard by this detective from Tumut named Binder. And he's got some offsider whose name I didn't catch, and Senior Sergeant Saunders has invited himself along too. So I'm sitting on the chair, and these guys are all basically leaning up against the wall, arms folded, trying to look intimidating. But I'm just sitting there smirking because all I can think about is having sex with Gregory, and if only they knew.

Anyway, Binder launches in, asking me how I came to discover the body. So I start to tell him how I like to go for an early-morning walk, and I was leaning down to pick wildflowers near the edge of the Pondage when I saw the body just floating there. And I notice as I talk that I am omitting completely a lot of the actual true details of the story—like Gregory, for example. I just totally refrain from mentioning him at all. And they're asking me if I touched or interfered with the body, and I'm like, 'Nope, absolutely no way,' because of course I know they are probably alluding to the missing hand. That is, the hand that Gregory broke off, the hand clutching the clump of stalks. And then Binder says, 'Sergeant Saunders tells me you identified the body as Miss Barker.' And I'm like, 'Yes.' And then he says, pretending to be all confused, 'But I understand you came here to replace Miss Barker?' And I'm like, 'That's right.' And he says, 'So how well did you actually know her?' I'm like, '*What?* I never met her.' And Binder says, 'Then how come you instantly identified the corpse?' And Saunders pipes up, 'Pretty frigging decomposed corpse at that.' And I'm like, 'Well, I just assumed. I put two and two together.' And Binder stares at me for a solid minute and then makes a long, long note in his notepad.

So then, when he's finally finished, he asks me if I can offer them any other details about Miss Barker. I'm like, 'I thought we just established that I never knew her.' And Binder says, 'Don't get smart with me. And while you're at it, wipe that smirk off your face. This isn't funny, in case you hadn't noticed.'

So I say, 'Well, I only know what some of the parents have told me. Which is mostly about her menstrual cycle.' And Binder says, 'Yeah, we're fully cognisant of her menstrual cycle.' So I say, 'Okay, but are you cognisant of the fact she had a miscarriage?' And he raises an eyebrow at this, and says, 'That's a new one. I haven't heard that.' So I say, 'Well, if you're looking for a reason why she jumped—' And he says, 'Jumped? You think she jumped?' And I'm like, 'Didn't they discharge water from the Reservoir last night? I'm assuming that's where the body came from.' And Binder says, 'Jumped off the Ridge, is that what you think? Sluice gates open, water discharged, body released into the Pondage?' So I say, 'Well, it certainly seems possible.' And Binder closes his notebook. He's like, 'You're very full of surmises for someone who didn't even know her.' And they all get up to go, and as they're filing out of there, Saunders turns and smirks at me. 'I'll tell you what, she was similar to you in this one respect,' he says. 'She was always with the love hickeys. But at least she used to try and cover them up.'

And the guys have a bit of a chuckle.

And then it hits me—Miss Barker and her floaty scarves. I thought it was her middle-aged dress sense. *But in fact she was covering up her love bites.*

I actually go cold. The hairs on my forearms stand on end. Because another thought suddenly dawns on me.

Miss Barker was on with Gregory.

Gregory gave her those love bites.

And in the same instant, I remember what he'd said only hours earlier in the Charger when he was going on about me having casual sex while intoxicated.

He said, 'The other one was just as bad.'

Meaning Miss Barker.

Of course.

I literally die a hundred times.

To be honest, I think I go into shock. I come over all clammy. A cold sweat breaks out on my forehead. I feel sick—sick to the pit of my stomach. I think to myself, *Okay, well, Miss Barker was on with Gregory. Also, Delores is having Josh's baby. Everything bad that could possibly happen is happening to me.*

Immediately the cops depart, I run and lock myself in the toilet and sit there hunched over, rocking back and forth, until Glenda starts banging on the door and yelling at me to get out of there.

I fling open the door and I'm like, 'WHAT?' And she looks at me and she obviously realises I've been crying, and she suddenly envelops me in this big suffocating hug. And she says, 'I'm sorry, Miss Mellett, this must be so hard for you. In the midst of our grief, we're forgetting that you're affected by it too.' It was very awkward and kind of sweaty and smothering, but I let it happen and actually it felt kind of nice that someone was finally considering how I felt about things. And then she says, 'Look, I've called the Department and a grief counsellor will be here on Monday. But someone really needs to speak to the children. And I just . . . I just don't think I can do it.'

And of course, cue the waterworks. So I pat her on the shoulder and I'm like, 'Don't worry, Glenda, of course I will talk to the children.'

And now she reverts to form and starts waving some Education Department guidelines at me like she doesn't entirely trust me with the task, and she's saying, 'Just explain it to them in a developmentally appropriate way. Be completely upfront and honest, but don't tell them more than they need to know. Let them know it's okay to cry or be sad or be angry—what's important is that we recognise our feelings and talk about them.'

And I'm like, 'Yup, yup. Thanks very much, Glenda, leave it with me.'

I have no idea how long I spent locked in the toilet, but somehow now it's after lunch, and the children are filing back into the classroom looking all mopey and forlorn and subdued. So I say to them, 'Okay, kids, gather round, form a circle, let's all sit on cushions on the floor. It's time we had a big, big talk about Miss Barker.'

So the children all come over and sit on the big, funny animal cushions that no doubt Miss Barker lovingly stitched by hand on her weekends. I get the little ones to come and sit really close to me, just so I can keep an eye on them, and to my surprise little Madison actually clambers onto my lap, which is sweet. And when everyone's settled, I begin.

'Kids, today is a very, very sad day for us. Miss Barker has been found in the Pondage. I'm afraid to say she is dead. Miss Barker is dead. Do you children all understand about death? Has anyone had a pet or a grandpa or a grandma or someone that has died?'

And so Ryan puts his hand up and says, 'My mum and dad died in a car crash, Miss.'

Thanks a lot, Ryan. Way to derail a class discussion. So I say, 'Actually, Ryan, I was really more asking the little kids, not you, but thank you for sharing.'

And then little Jaden puts his hand up and tells us a long story about his dead mice with lots of unnecessary detail about their tumours which has everyone completely grossing out, and all the time there is snot pouring out his nose and finally I can't stand it and I cut him off and tell him to go and get a tissue.

And then Rose and Brody want to talk about the massacred chickens, basically so they can whip themselves up into a state of competitive tweeny hysteria, so I nip that in the bud and say, 'Yes, but really they were only chickens, and let's face it, you probably eat chicken every night and don't even think about it.'

So then I say, 'Let's get back to Miss Barker. Is anyone wondering what on earth she was doing in the Pondage in the first place?'

The kids just stare at me, but finally little Benjamin says, 'Swimming?'

Which just totally cracked me up. Totes inappropes, I know, but his timing could not have been more perfect if he was Jack Benny. I am laughing so hard, I am clutching my stomach, I am practically weeping. Finally, I manage to compose myself, and I say, 'Thank you, Benjamin, but I don't actually think Miss Barker was swimming.' And then I look around and I say, 'Any other thoughts?'

And Sarah, one of the older girls, says: 'Did she drown?'

To which I respond, 'Duh. Obviously she drowned, Sarah. But my question is why was she even in the Pondage? I mean, I actually saw her body and she had clothes on. Normal clothes.'

And Oliver says, 'Maybe she fell in?'

And I'm like, 'Bingo! Give the boy a banana. Did everyone hear what Oliver said? He said maybe Miss Barker fell in. I think we're getting warmer. Any other ideas? Like, maybe if we try to think where she could have fallen from?'

I am trying to lead the conversation around as delicately as I can to suicide. But the kids absolutely won't take the bait. They keep proposing more and more ludicrous ideas. She fell from a tree, a plane, a hot-air balloon, a rocket ship. I mean, it was nuts. Finally I cut them off and I say, 'Maybe she fell from the Ridge. Did anyone think about that?'

And this thought seems to genuinely shock them. I guess they all know the Ridge, they know how scary and high up it is and what a long way down to the dark, cold water. So now I put on a pretend-puzzled face, and I say, 'But why would she fall from the Ridge? Everyone knows you have to stay away from the edge, right? Do you think Miss Barker knew she had to stay away from the edge? Of course she did—she's a teacher. So why would Miss

Barker, a fully qualified primary school teacher, have gone too close to the edge if she knew better than anyone that you have to stay away from the edge? It doesn't make sense, does it?'

Cue a hundred increasingly implausible suggestions as to why Miss Barker went too close to the edge. She was trying to get better phone reception. She was taking a selfie and wanted to see more of the water. She dropped a lolly wrapper and as she went to pick it up, it blew over the edge. A lion was chasing her. A meteorite was hurtling towards her. And then finally Ryan says, 'Maybe somebody pushed her.'

Well, all the kids just completely turn on him. Totally shout him down. Why would anyone push Miss Barker off the Ridge? Everybody loved Miss Barker! That is the craziest idea they've ever heard! Ryan is a stupid idiot! And so finally I intervene, and I say, 'Guess what, kids? You're all wrong. Miss Barker actually jumped off.'

They all turn to me then, their little faces puckering in disbelief.

'That's what the cops think. They said Miss Barker was sad because her baby died, and sometimes women get a bit unhinged, a bit crazy, when things like that happen. I think it's partly the hormones. And because she was sad, she jumped off the Ridge.'

But some of the kids cry out, 'Miss Barker didn't have a baby!'

So I explain, 'In her tummy. A baby was growing in her tummy, but it died.'

But still the children protest—they would not believe me. Miss Barker couldn't have had a baby in her tummy because the Riley-Campbells' mummy has a baby inside her and she has a big fat tummy, and Miss Barker didn't have a big fat tummy. So finally, worn down by all those shrill voices, I lose patience and say, 'Look, don't shoot the messenger, I'm just repeating what the cops said. But there's lots of things about Miss Barker that you kids don't know the half of. I'm not going to go into details because that's not appropriate, so let's just leave it at that.'

I glance at Ryan then, because I'm thinking about Gregory—in particular, I'm thinking about Miss Barker and Gregory and Miss Barker's love bites. And Ryan is looking at me, very direct, straight in the eyes, and we hold that gaze between us for several long moments until finally I look away. Because suddenly I realise that Ryan knows a lot more about things than he lets on. I can't describe it, but his look seemed to convey a silent message of understanding and support. It was as if he was trying to communicate to me: *I know. I know everything. It's all right. It's all right.*

So anyway, the bell finally goes and the kids file out, and just as I'm tidying up a bit, who should suddenly descend on me but the Praying Mantis. That's right, Friar Hernandez pays a pastoral visit, just to cap off a great day. He sweeps in, closes the door behind him and says, 'I came as soon as I heard. How are you? Are you all right?' And I'm like, 'I'm okay,' and he's like, 'Are you sure?', and I'm like, 'Yeah, really, I'm fine. I mean, it's been pretty harrowing, but yeah, I'm okay.' And he's like, 'Can I say a prayer or something?' And I'm like, 'Uh . . . no thanks.'

And then he flops down in a chair and buries his head in his hands. He seems absolutely distraught. He's groaning and rocking and muttering to himself, and then finally he lifts his head and he says, 'Oh, Eleanor. I've been struggling, really struggling, with whether or not to tell you this.'

Immediately my hackles go up. I'm on full alert. I'm super wary. So I say, 'Tell me what? Is this about Miss Barker?' And for a nanosecond, I glimpse a flicker of confusion as if he has no idea what Miss Barker has to do with anything. Then he says, 'Oh, Miss Barker, poor thing, how sad, no. No, it's nothing to do with her. It's to do with me. And you.'

And then he says, 'There's nothing for it but for me to come right out and say it. I am infected. You have infected me.'

This is actual fact. I am quoting him verbatim.

'*You have infected me.*'

So I just look at him and I say, 'What the fuck are you talking about?'

And then he's saying, 'Oh, I don't blame you. I blame myself. I was ill-prepared. I should have fasted. I should have used holy water. But no, I saw a need and I thought I could do it, and now I have prostate cancer. Do you see?'

I am shaking my head, in disbelief more than anything. So he leans right into my face and he says, '*It departed you and it entered me.*'

I go icy calm, which is what I do in moments of extreme duress. I say to him, 'Let me get this straight. You have prostate cancer?'

And he says, 'I've just come from my urologist this minute.'

'You think I gave it to you?'

'Yes, unwittingly.'

I take a deep breath and I say, 'Listen, mister. Do you have any idea how common prostate cancer is in men your age? Talk to your urologist. I did not give it to you. The cancer did not depart my body and enter yours. And, *fyi*, Friar Hernandez, just by the way, cancer is many things but one thing it isn't is *contagious*.'

This is when he got scary. Up until now, he'd been a bit mad but mostly pathetic. All dishevelled and sweaty and loser-ish. But now he seems actually certifiably, dangerously insane. Like a psychopath. His eyes have this manic gleam, and he's saying, '*It's the demon, don't you understand? The demon that I cast out of you has entered me. I was vulnerable, and it saw that I was vulnerable—*'

At which point, I shout at the top of my voice, 'PLEASE DEPART.'

Except not so politely.

And then I shout, 'DO ME A FAVOUR AND KINDLY STAY AWAY FROM ME FOREVER.'

Also not so politely.

But he just stands there, taking big deep breaths like he's preparing for a long swim underwater. And then he says, 'Maybe you're right.'

I don't say anything. Because I have come to realise that every time I say something, this guy seems to feed off it somehow or use it against me. So I stay mute while he edges around me like I'm some kind of tarantula. And he says in a very low voice, 'When I look at you, I can see it there still. Oh yes. I can see it still residing there within you. So perhaps I wasn't entirely successful ... '

I shove him as hard as I can—I actually can't believe the strength I suddenly find within myself—I shove him out the door so hard he crashes backwards into the lockers in the corridor, and then I slam the door and I lock it. I lean against it with my full body weight, breathing hard. To be honest, I'm surprised at myself. Also I'm wondering whether I've hurt him. I can hear him whimpering and moaning out in the corridor, but I don't want to open the door and check because I suspect he might be tricking me. Sure enough, after a while, I hear him creeping away.

Only in Talbingo, folks.

Unbelievable.

So when I finally pull myself together after all that, I get my bag and I unlock the classroom door and I'm on my way out when I realise Glenda is still in her office, just sitting quietly at her desk. So even though the last thing I feel like is a chin-wag with Glenda, I do the decent thing and pop my head in and say goodnight.

And she turns to look at me, and I can see she has been sitting there crying for a good long time, because her eyes are red and her face is all puffy and swollen. And she says, 'What did he want?'

I say, 'Who?'

'Friar Hernandez,' says Glenda. 'Who do you think?'

'I don't know, he wanted to say a prayer or something.'

She doesn't say anything to this, just sits there, so I wait for a moment to see if she's going to volunteer anything else. I notice the bin has been emptied and the strand of my hair has been removed from the filing cabinet handle and the whole room stinks of anti-bacterial spray. After a few minutes seem to have ticked by or possibly a lifetime or two, filled only by the sound of Glenda sniffling into her sodden hanky, I say in a loud, cheerful voice, 'Okay, well, have a nice evening, Glenda! I'll see you tomorrow.'

And then she says, 'It's a very odd coincidence, isn't it, Miss Mellett, that you should find the body.'

Well, after the day I've had, this really takes the biscuit. I suddenly feel immensely weary, just exhausted from all the nonsense I am continually expected to endure in this backwater. I turn and I say, 'What are you suggesting, Glenda? That in my desperation to secure this position, I murdered my predecessor?'

And Glenda says, 'Well, let's face it, you've never had a single nice thing to say about her.'

A horrible silence descends between us. Then I turn and leave.

Okay so I'm sound asleep and I'm dreaming that I'm making out with Gregory in the back seat of his Charger. Suddenly I think, Wait a minute, if we're in the back seat, who the hell is driving?? And I look up, and somehow I realise it's his dad driving and his mum beside him in the front seat—also Ryan's in the back seat with us, squished up against the door, playing on his Nintendo. So that's embarrassing, given Gregory and I are practically having sex. And I'm trying to get a good look at the parents, because I'm curious, but all I can see is the backs of their heads and the dad's fingers tap-tap-tapping on the steering wheel. Meanwhile I'm starting to become aware of this strange erratic rumbling noise, and I'm thinking, What is that? Because it sounds familiar, and the familiarity is making me uneasy. And then I see it—it's the bus again, the horrible stinking bus I got stuck behind, but now it's coming straight for us on the highway. But the dad doesn't seem alarmed, in fact he doesn't even seem to see it because he's certainly not taking any evasive action, and I'm thinking, Of course! This must be how they got themselves killed in a car crash! And then I think, Hang on, does that mean I'm about to die too?? So I'm gesturing wildly at the bus and trying to warn them but I can't seem to form the words, and next I hear this terrible asthmatic squeal as the bus slams on its air brakes, and I think, This is it, this is how I'm going to die, how ludicrous—

And then I wake up. With a start, like they do in the movies. I lie there in bed for a moment before it dawns on me. The dream is over but I can still hear a rumbling noise. And it's coming from outside.

I get out of bed and creep to the lounge-room window, which is the window that faces the street. And even before I pull the curtain aside, I know what I'm about to see.

It's the bus, of course. The horrible stinking bus.

I swear to God.

Parked right outside my house on the street.

Its engine is idling, really rough, like it's got the wrong fuel, and every now and then it makes a kind of lurching sound, as if someone's giving the accelerator a bit of juice. Its headlights are on, and its interior lights too, but they're very dim and kind of bluish. From what I can make out, it seems to be empty. Nor can I see any driver, but I guess there has to be one because now the door opens, by which I mean the bus door.

It opens like it's expecting a passenger.

And for some reason, this just freaks me out. I mean, I'm seriously unnerved anyway, owing to the day I've had, but the way this bus door slides open, complete with wheezy sound effects, this just spooks the bejesus out of me.

So immediately I pull the curtain shut. Then I run to the front door and make sure all the locks are bolted. Likewise the back door. Then I stand there stock-still in the hallway. My heart is thumping so loud, I swear I can actually hear it.

Ba-boom. Ba-boom. Ba-boom.

So I try to talk some sense to myself. I say, Eleanor, seriously, this is just a bus. This is just a bus which happens to be parked outside your house. Are you now developing a phobia of public transport?

Okay, you've had a bad experience with a bus. Possibly this exact same bus, although admittedly it's hard to be sure in the darkness. But when you really examine that previous incident closely, was it not caused by your own stupidity and impatience to get home and crack open the sav blanc asap?

True . . .

But why does (possibly) this very same bus now materialise outside my house in the middle of the fucking night?

Harassment, that's what this is.

And at the very least, if this is not direct harassment then it's extremely inconsiderate of the driver to be idling his rattly old rust bucket directly outside my house at such an ungodly hour. (Okay, it is only 11.30 pm, but still, I was sound asleep having sex with Gregory.) So I decide to confront him. In my nightie. I surprise myself sometimes with my assertiveness.

I go to the front door and undo all the locks, then I open it. The first thing that hits me is the smell. It smells noxious, like it's emitting all sorts of toxic exhaust fumes. Also, the rumbling is now much louder, interspersed with the odd clunk and rattle—seriously, this bus needs its muffler attended to at the very least.

And for what seems the longest time, I just stand there on the porch and stare at it. Because now I am struggling with two equally strong but conflicting desires:

1. I want to run back inside, lock the doors and hide under the bed.
2. I want to board that bus.

It's like the feeling you get sometimes with heights—standing on the edge of the Ridge, for example. It is simultaneously extremely scary and yet somehow weirdly compelling. There's a pull, I guess, is the best way to describe it.

Likewise with this bus. It's something about the fact that it opened its door—it feels like it opened for me. Consequently, I feel an anxiety not to keep it waiting. Like, if I test its patience by dilly-dallying too much, it might leave without me. Yet, at the same time, I cannot seem to get my feet to move. It requires an enormous exertion of will for me to finally step off that porch and onto the path. And even then, it's a weirdly slow, stilted, stiff-legged walk, like a paraplegic's first steps or something. Part of my brain is trying to hold me back is what it feels like. Part of my brain is so desperate for me not to board that bus, it is trying to get me to forget how to walk. Like I suddenly have no notion of what my knees are for.

So with my nightie flapping about me in the wind, I'm staggering down the path towards the bus. And as I get within about a metre of it, I reach out towards it and the door slides shut. Very abrupt, with a nasty metallic sound like it fully intended to take off my fingers. Then the whole bus gives a kind of shudder, like someone's walked over its grave. It moves off very heavily, working through its gears, and lumbers around the corner into Pether Street, scraping up against a street sign in the process. I can no longer see it now, but I can hear it, which is almost worse, lurching and wheezing through the back streets. Finally it reaches the highway—I can tell by the whining sound of its engines ramping up to full throttle.

I stand there listening for a solid ten minutes till I'm not sure I can even hear it anymore. Then I realise my feet have gone numb on the cold ground, so I hurry back inside, pull all the locks across and bury myself under the blankets. But I can't sleep, so I get up and write it all down. And now the strange thing is, I'm wondering if I didn't actually dream the whole thing. Something was certainly weird about it all.

It's getting so that I don't trust my own consciousness.

Is that mets? Is that what brain metastases feel like?

I can't afford to think like this. I need to sleep. I need to get some actual sleep.

I just had a thought. An actual rational thought.

If the street sign is damaged, then it actually happened.

If the street sign is not damaged, then I must have halluci-
nated the whole thing.

I'm going to put my coat on and run up and check.

- - - - - - - - - - - - - - - - - - - -

The street sign is not damaged.

I am going mad.

So anyone might think I'd had enough drama for the week, but in fact there was more to come. Thank God it's Friday, is all I can say. And the irony is that I came to Talbingo to escape the stress! Because stress is just like the worst possible thing for breast cancer. And on a scale of one to being carted off to the nuthouse in a straitjacket, let's just say I am well and truly into the red section. I mean, the needle is probably spinning around and around like it does in cartoons. Like the altimeter in a cockpit when a plane goes into a graveyard spiral.

So my day begins at dawn. For some reason, I'm suddenly wide awake, even after having seriously about two hours sleep max. I get up and go to the window and peer out. The kangaroos are moving down to the water and, as I'm watching them, I catch a glimpse of movement in the Pondage. It's hard to see because of the mist, but there seems to be a small figure wading waist-deep. And even from this distance, I can tell that it's Ryan.

I think, *Shit! What's he doing?* I throw some clothes on, and I hurry down to the edge of the Pondage. And there he is, quite a way in now, right up to his chest in fact. I call out to him, 'Ryan! What are you doing?' But he doesn't seem to hear me. And then I realise that he seems to have a small fishing net in his hand and he is ducking down under the water and then re-emerging with the net filled with mud and Pondage crap. He sifts through it quickly, tips it out and goes under again for more. The air temperature, I might add, is about four degrees Celsius. I know from experience that the Pondage water would be practically zero. I mean, how can he stand it? Why hasn't the boy got hypothermia? It's insane!

So next time he pops his head up out of the water, I scream out to him again, louder this time. And he looks up and sees me and gives a little wave, then just continues sifting through the contents of his net. So I holler at him, *'Ryan! Come out! I don't think it's safe in there!'* But he just ignores me. I realise then that, as the only adult present, I have no other option but to go in and drag him out. So in I go, fully clothed, like an idiot.

Immediately my legs start cramping from the cold, like they did yesterday. Also, I have a lot of clothes on and the weight of them waterlogged is pulling me under. And the bottom of the Pondage is so boggy—it's a huge effort to drag my feet up out of the mud. It's getting worse the deeper I go, till the mud actually pulls one of my Blundstones off and then, with the next step, the other one. So now I've lost my favourite boots—thanks a lot, Ryan! And all the while I'm struggling out to him, Ryan's busily ducking under water and scooping, then examining his net, tipping out the contents and scooping again. I keep screaming out his name, but it's almost like he doesn't hear me. I'm becoming more and more breathless with the exertion, and I suddenly realise with a jolt of horror that there's a very good chance I could drown out here. And one nanosecond after I have this realisation, I go under.

I'm not sure what happened. I must have stepped into a hole. And although I excel at holding my breath, I wasn't prepared this time, and I have nothing, no breath in my lungs at all. I thrash around underwater, trying to fight my way to the surface, but my clothes just keep pulling me down again.

I manage to pull off my duffle coat and that action frees me enough to fight my way to the surface for a quick gasp of air, and then I go under again. Now I'm frantic. I'm not even sure that Ryan has noticed my predicament. I try to pull off my jumper next—it's the big heavy cable-knit that Mum knitted me, and as usual she's done the neckband too tight and it's all caught up around my face like it's trying to smother me, but I know I have to get it off or it will drown me. I'm completely fucking panicking. The more I struggle, the tighter the jumper seems to wrap itself around my head, and now my arms are all entangled in it. My brain is screaming for oxygen. I can't stand it, I can't stand the burning, bursting feeling in my lungs and the terrible, terrible sense of panic and I think, well, maybe it's just easier to breathe—but some last vestige of survival instinct screams, NO, ELEANOR,

WHATEVER YOU DO, DON'T TRY TO BREATHE!
IF YOU BREATHE UNDERWATER, YOU'LL DIE!

So I breathe. Underwater.

The next thing I know, I'm lying on the shore amid all the reeds and duck poo and I'm vomiting up water and bile and tadpoles and duckling feathers. I look up and there's Ryan standing over me, and there's a shaft of golden sunlight behind him because the sun has just come up over the mountains. It's like I'm seeing some kind of vision—Ryan the Exalted, the Glorious. And when I finally get my breath, I gasp out, 'How did you do it? How did you save me?' Because I cannot imagine how he managed to pull me in, him being just a kid and me being all tangled up in my waterlogged clothes. But he just shrugs and says, 'Well, it wasn't that deep. I don't know why you didn't just stand up. I think you were having some kind of panic attack or something.' And when he says those words 'panic attack', I feel this wave of indescribable rage and anger. Because that's what Josh always used to accuse me of: having panic attacks as some kind of attention-seeking device. Even though I had every legitimate reason to be panicking, i.e. like the time I locked myself in the boot of the car and Josh didn't even notice I was missing. So I say to Ryan, 'Of course I was panicking! I was worried you would drown! What were you doing in there anyway? It was a stupid, stupid thing to do!' And then he tells me he was trying to find Miss Barker's hand.

So apparently word is out among the tweenies that Miss Barker's corpse was missing a hand, and Ryan's being all junior detective: 'Why would she be missing a hand? Two hands, yes, I can understand that. Someone's trying to disguise her identity. But one hand? It doesn't make sense!' And I say, 'Maybe a fish ate it. Did you think of that?' And he says, incredulously, 'A fish ate an entire hand?' So I say, 'Well, maybe it was several fish. A whole bunch of fish.' But he still doesn't buy it. I'm getting a bit fed up now because the last thing I want to talk about is Miss Barker's hand, especially since Ryan's actual brother, who I'm in love with, is the one that, uh, shall we say, removed it from her. So I'm like, 'Look, Ryan, why don't we just allow the police to do their work. In the meantime, stay out of the Pondage. It's too dangerous.'

And suddenly I become aware of the fact that I am shivering violently because I am in fact tremendously cold, and that is because I am clad only in my muddy underwear, which is rather embarrassing. I have no idea what happened to my jeans. So I stand up and I say to him very sternly, 'Listen, Ryan, you are not to tell a soul about this, all right? If you tell anyone, I am going to make sure there are very serious repercussions for you. Like maybe a foster home or a juvenile detention centre.' And he gets a bit upset about this but he finally agrees, and then I run home in the misty dawn, praying that nobody sees me. It would confirm everyone's opinion of me, that's for sure, to see me scarpering across the golf course in my muddy undies.

I stood under the shower till the hot water ran out, vomiting up more frog spawn and leaf matter. Then I put on my pyjamas and called in sick. There's no way I can face another day of school today. Luckily Glenda wasn't in yet, so I just left a message on the answering machine.

I've tried to lay low over the weekend. Mostly I've just stayed in bed, obsessing about Gregory—in particular, about Gregory and Miss Barker. I keep trying to get the evidence straight in my head, but lately my head is just so muddled and confused. I mean, do I have any actual evidence? A) Saunders reckons Miss Barker used to have love bites. B) She wore a lot of floaty scarves.

THAT DOESN'T MEAN FOR ONE MINUTE THAT SHE WAS ON WITH GREGORY.

And then I remember my other piece of 'evidence', if you can call it that, which is what Gregory said in the Charger that morning when he was banging on about me lacking a moral compass.

He said, '*The other one was just as bad.*'

But what does that even mean? The other *what* was just as bad? Why did I immediately think he meant the other teacher, as in Miss Barker? And did I even hear him correctly?

For example, I'm pretty sure me remembering or half remembering what he said would not be admissible in court, because basically it's called 'hearsay'.

Of course, thinking about Gregory saying all those horrible things to me just makes me feel like shit. It's very hard to feel okay about yourself when someone says such terrible things to you. I can barely even remember what he said, but I know that it was bad—very, very bad. I remember the words 'moral compass', and I remember the word 'systemic' and the word 'intoxicated', and mostly I remember him saying 'the other one was just as bad'. But some part of my brain seems to have blotted out the rest of it. Whatever he said was so hideous that my brain just had to obliterate it, or else die.

About two o'clock on Sunday the phone starts ringing. By which I mean the landline. Of course I just try to ignore it. I think it's probably Mum, and I can't bear to talk to Mum at the moment, because it means having to try to pretend everything's fine and she would see right through me in about five seconds. So I just let it ring, hoping Mum might think I'm out being busy and active and fulfilled in my new life. It rings out but then it starts ringing again, and this repeats every few minutes. Finally, I begin to think, well, maybe something's happened, perhaps there's some kind of emergency. So I answer it.

'Eleanor?' says this nervy little tremulous voice. 'Have you forgotten?'

'Who is this?' I ask.

'It's Daphne,' she says. I stay silent, but I have a creeping feeling going up my spine. It's the Little Sparrow, of course, the strange shrunken woman I met outside the church that time the Praying Mantis exorcised my demons.

173

'Have you forgotten?' she asks again.

'Forgotten what?'

'The decoupage workshop is this afternoon. Remember the leaflet I gave you?'

I actually bark with laughter. Like that's really what I want to do right now, Daphne. Decoupage things. Glue pictures for therapy and then cover them with varnish, like I'm in a sheltered workshop.

'We thought it might be nice to decoupage a small box to give Miss Barker's family, possibly for her ashes if they choose to cremate her, or just as a keepsake box to hold small, treasured mementoes of her life,' says Little Sparrow. 'It would be so much more meaningful if everyone who knew her contributed a picture or decorative detail of some kind.'

'I didn't know her,' I say. 'I just found the body.'

There's a silence on the other end of the line.

'Nevertheless, you have a connection,' she says.

I hang up on her.

To be honest, I immediately feel bad that I did that. Poor Little Sparrow and her decoupage, trying to be helpful. She sounded so needy, almost pathetic. I picture her alone in the church hall, everything laid out in readiness. Would anyone show up? Maybe no one would show up. I mean, let's face it, she was reduced to ringing me, of all people. Also, I feel bad about this habit I have of hanging up on folk. I need to stop doing that. I do it all the time, whenever things get uncomfortable.

So I go back to bed but, as I'm lying there, I can't get rid of this idea that Daphne's all alone in the church hall, vainly hoping someone will show up. I feel so bad about it that I pull on my clothes, brush my teeth and go over there and, sure enough, it's exactly as I imagined it! Daphne sitting all alone at a big table, surrounded by piles of *Women's Weeklies* and pots of glue and lacquer, bravely keeping herself busy cutting out pictures from the magazines. It's heart-breaking. Nobody, not one single person in this lousy town, has shown up to her decoupage workshop.

That fact alone should have given me pause. But one thing I'm noticing: I don't seem to be too good these days at picking up on warning signs.

The floorboards of the church hall creak as I enter, and this seems to startle her. For a moment I actually think she's about to dive under the table. But then she recovers when she realises it's me, and she smiles up at me hopefully. She's obviously surprised, even delighted, to see me and I feel good about myself for once in my life. It's not hard to be a nice person.

I should try it more often.

Immediately she thrusts a pile of magazines at me, and a pair of tiny plastic scissors, the sort you might give pre-schoolers.

'Let's get cracking,' she says. 'I'm just going through all of these to find anything that seems to resonate with me when I think about Miss Barker.'

As if to demonstrate, she licks her index finger and proceeds to flick briskly through a magazine, frowning occasionally if something displeases her. Suddenly she stops, rests her hand on a picture and closes her eyes in concentration. Then she opens her eyes and sets to cutting. Her trembling little hands shake so much, she can barely manage her tiny scissors. I look at the picture she's cutting out, and my heart sinks. She's clearly a loony. No wonder no one has bothered turning up. It's an instructional diagram illustrating how best to shape your eyebrows.

I look at the pile she's cut out already. There are pictures of Kim and Kanye and refrigerators and product shots of fabric softeners and deodorant and several pictures involving various ways to serve cauliflower. All hacked out haphazardly as if by somebody going cold turkey off their medication.

She glances up at me. 'Better get a wriggle on,' she says, in her wavering little voice. 'We have a lot to get done this afternoon.' And she indicates the small wooden box, about the size of a box of tissues, which apparently we are to decoupage with pictures of Kim and Kanye and cauliflower bakes etc. It dawns on me that I'm going to have to take charge here and try to steer the decoupage into something half-way appropriate, especially if this is going to be presented to Miss Barker's family. So I open up a *Women's Weekly*, and set to work. I'm looking for flowers and laughing children and hearts and bows and ribbons. But once I start looking, I seem to be immediately afflicted with a variation of Daphne's problem. The worst possible images seem to resonate with me. It's not that they're inappropriate exactly—they're too appropriate. I find myself cutting out tampon ads and pictures of newborn babies and, wherever I can, I'm dismembering hands. I get particularly excited about a nail polish ad, because it offers such a perfect image of a female hand. It takes me ages to cut around all the fingers because I'm trying to demonstrate to Daphne that we need to take a bit of care here.

When I've finished, I place the hand on the top of the pile of pictures. And Daphne falls upon it in raptures. 'This is perfect!' she exclaims. 'This is exactly what I've been looking for!' And she immediately seizes her glue brush and starts gluing it onto the top of the box. But she's so trembly and rushed, she's botching it up completely. The hand is too big so she has to fold the fingers over the edge of the box, but in trying to do this, she's causing all these creases and bubbles to appear. And everybody knows that with decoupage, there's two simple rules: no creases, and absolutely no fucking bubbles. So then she's trying to smooth them all out, but

177

she's so agitated that she tears one of the fingers. And given that the picture has taken me about twenty minutes to cut out so meticulously, I completely lose my shit. 'Careful!' I practically yell at her. 'You see what you've done? You've totally wrecked it!'

Well, I feel terrible because she crumples completely. She's literally a puddle on the floor. 'I'm useless!' she's blubbering. 'I'm useless at everything!'

'No, you're not useless,' I say, and I go around and sit next to her and sort of pat her on her back, which is so bony it scares me so I stop patting her. 'You were just a bit rough, that's all. I've done a lot of this craft stuff, and anything involving glue and paper, trust me, years of experience, you have to be super careful.'

And now she sighs a fluttery little sigh and she leans her head against me, which is weird and freaks me out a bit, but I gingerly place a comforting arm around her shoulder. 'It's just that I feel like I'm failing her,' she says.

'Failing who?' I ask.

'Miss Barker.'

I get a little cold chill up my neck.

'She's stuck, you see. I can feel it. She doesn't want to go.'

'Stuck?' I say.

'That's what I feel. Either she's confused or angry or maybe she's left something behind, but she's not going anywhere.'

Meanwhile I'm staring at the hand on the box. I know exactly what Miss Barker has left behind, currently submerged in mud and eel poo at the bottom of the Pondage.

'And I promised her,' bleats Daphne. 'As soon as I heard that you'd found her in the Pondage. I said, "Miss Barker, I will help you transition." Because that's what I do, you see. That's what I'm here for.'

By now, I'm totally wishing that I'd never got out of bed to answer that phone. (Why does anyone ever get out of bed? Nothing good can come of it.) Also I'm noticing that she seems to have the heating in the hall up super high, because the atmosphere is stifling, thick with glue fumes.

'People don't realise that spirits sometimes need assistance,' she's saying. 'But of course, after what they've been through, they're terribly nervous. Not to mention disoriented. They sometimes require a firm hand. But in this case, nothing I do seems to make any difference.'

I actually flinch when she says 'firm hand', and let out a kind of nervous giggle. Now she leans forward very close. I get the familiar whiff of eau de cologne and mothballs. Clearly

Daphne must suspend herself in a wardrobe in between appearances.

'I hope you won't take this the wrong way,' she whispers, 'but I think it's you.'

'Me?'

'You're the problem.'

'Why?' I cry, immediately on the defensive. 'What have I ever done to Miss Barker?'

'It's the children. She's worried about the children. Because of course, she's devoted to them.'

I stare at her.

A drop of sweat literally falls off my eyebrow.

She's got me. She's totally got me. I can't argue this one.

Because of course Miss Barker has every reason to be worried about the children. I couldn't possibly be a less competent teacher. I'm never prepared. I'm always handing out the same old worksheets. Sometimes I don't even check if they're age-appropriate. The other day the littlies were up in arms because I gave them a worksheet on long division. I'm like, 'Don't be such babies, at least have a go at it!' Big mistake.

Tears, threats, tantrums ensued. And the whole time, unbeknownst to me, Miss B. is wafting about in the rafters observing all this! Let me say, it's a very weird uncomfortable feeling to know that ghosts, spirits, whatever, have been spying on you. And then complaining about you to anyone who will listen, namely Daphne.

'You know what?' I say. 'Tell Miss Barker not to worry. Okay, there's been a few teething problems, but once I get them straightened out—'

I stop with a jolt because I'm remembering that Miss Barker was on with Gregory.

~~(Possibly.)~~

~~(Maybe not.)~~

~~(Probably.)~~

(Most likely.)

A horrible thought occurs to me.

If Miss Barker knows about the worksheets, what else does she know?

I'm creeped out. I actually shudder. The phrase 'gross invasion of privacy' springs to mind. Just because someone's dead does not give them the right to poke their nose into someone else's business, and I say as much to Daphne. It's my classroom now, so get over yourself, Miss B. And another thing: okay, I'm pretty used to copping the blame for everything in this town, but I'm buggered if I'm going to accept responsibility for Miss Barker rattling around groaning and moaning when she should just do us all a favour and skedaddle off to whatever celestial pastures await her.

Well, Daphne is apparently not used to this kind of forthright talk and from all the lip-trembling that's going on, I assume she's about to dissolve into tears again. But instead, she surprises me. I feel her tiny torso stiffen and she takes a deep shaky breath.

'I don't blame you for what you say because you can't help it,' she says. 'You have a sickness. The cells of your body are turning against you.'

Let me just take a moment to think about this.

The rational part of what's left of my brain says that Little
Sparrow and Friar Hernandez have been gossiping about me,
and what she said simply represents her extremely minimal
understanding of cancer. But the irrational part of my brain
(which is most of it) doesn't like it at all. I think back to that
doctor's drawing of my stupid cells piling up on top of each
other, and I wonder, Is that what the doctor meant? Are all
those infinitesimal cells, unique to me, the essence of me,
that go together to make me, now under instruction to terminate me? To self-destruct? To scuttle the sub and leave it
rusting on the ocean floor? Am I so despicable a person that
even my own body can't stand me?

I totally can't afford to think like this.

Of course, I got out of there straight away. I wasn't hanging around for more insights from Daphne. Besides, it was literally 600 degrees in there, like a hot yoga studio. Also, the fumes from her eau de cologne were making me nauseous.

Once I step outside and the cold mountain air hits me, my queasiness subsides and I realise that I'm actually quite hungry. So since I'm up and dressed and out and about, I decide to go to the shop and stock up on my usual, by which I mean Coke, Jatz crackers, and a family-size block of Dairy Milk chocolate. I say hi to Janelle, but (am I imagining this?) she seems a little cool towards me. A little thin-lipped and judgy in her demeanour. I try to think what in particular she could be so frosty about, but I don't think I've done anything especially terrible since the Parent–Teacher Night. Except find Miss Barker's body in the Pondage. Surely these hicks don't blame me for that?

And just as I'm coming out of the shop with my supplies, I see this group of young people piling out of a couple of four-wheel drives. I guess they're about my age or maybe a bit younger and clearly they're just passing through, on their way back from the snow. And they all look so happy, like life is so good, and they're clowning around and cracking up at some joke they have going. They pay me no attention; I don't think they even really see me. But I just stop in my tracks and stare at them. They represent everything I want and don't have. They radiate health and youth and happiness and good times and fun and laughter and friendship. And on top of the afternoon I've just had, the sight of them radiating all that fucking sunshine sends me plunging right into the abyss. Because I've been robbed of all that. It flew out the window the day the cancer demon came knocking at my door. Because somehow, through an unhappy combination of personal weakness, bad genes, bad living and bad luck, instead of slamming the door right in the face of that hoary old devil, apparently I opened wide and welcomed him in.

So I came home and cried for about three hours.

Maybe it wasn't such a good idea to chuck out my antidepressants.

Now I've cracked open a bottle of wine. I'm trying to devise a plan, is what I'm trying to do. I need to dig myself out of this abyss.

Because I've been here before and it's bad. In my experience, you have to treat it exactly the same way James Franco did when that giant boulder fell on him when he was canyoning.

You have to do what it takes to get out, even if it means drinking your own urine and sawing off your arm with a blunt pocket knife.

First up, ask yourself, where does the misery spring from?

Is it this horrible job?

Certainly it's partly this horrible job.

So why don't I just quit? Why put up with all this crap? There is absolutely nothing to stop me packing up the car, and hotfooting it out of here. I don't owe anyone anything. I hate it here. Everyone is either mad or horrible. Those are the two options: mad or horrible. Even Gregory, and he is the best thing about this place, is mad and horrible—and besides, he was on with Miss Barker.

Okay, let's seriously think about this. I guess if I walk out, it's safe to assume that the Education Department will never give me another job, ever. I mean, let's face it, they'd only just started employing me again. But maybe I could legitimately claim mental health issues? I mean, I did actually find a dead body— surely that could justify an abrupt departure. And anyway, when I really think about it, do I even want to be a teacher anymore? I don't think I'm cut out for it. I have no patience. I used to have patience, but I don't anymore. I just seem to be in a permanent state of irritability all the time. Those whiny little voices make me want to rip my own head off.

Would it be running away? By which I mean, *am I running away from my problems?*

Yes. That's exactly what I am doing. And it wouldn't be the first time.

Oh, fuck it. I'm going.

I actually packed. I packed up all my things and I was sitting on my suitcase trying to do up the zipper when I heard a knock on the front door.

Hope springs eternal, as my father used to say. I was, of course, predictably, hoping it was Gregory. Hence the eagerness with which I threw the door open. Unfortunately, there's Ryan standing on my doorstep.

He's keen to make cupcakes. Apparently he and Miss Barker used to make cupcakes on a regular basis, and supposedly I'd promised him we'd make cupcakes also. 'And don't forget,' he reminds me by way of emotional blackmail, 'I did actually save your life in the Pondage the other day.' I look at him and I think, Okay, well, fair enough. I owe this kid some cupcakes. Nevertheless I'll hot-foot it out of here just as soon as we yank said cupcakes out of oven. So I let him in.

We whip up some cake batter and he pours it into the patty pans, then we stick them on a tray and into the oven. I set the timer for twenty minutes. And then Ryan says to me, 'Do you want to do it now?'

I say, 'Do it? What do you mean, do it?'

And he's like, 'You know. Do it. Miss Barker and me used to do it while the cupcakes cooked.'

I think, *Am I hearing the boy correctly?*

'Do you mean ... seriously ... *do it*?' I ask him. I am somewhat incredulous to say the least.

And he nods, with a silly little smirk on his face.

'Have sex?' I clarify.

He nods again, more smirking.

'Are you telling me you had sex with Miss Barker???' I cry in a loud shrill voice. I mean, I am completely horrified. And obviously my reaction freaks Ryan out, because he stops smirking and he goes bright red. 'She made me!' he says.

And then he starts blubbering, and he's saying, 'You won't send me to the boys' home, will you?' And I say to him, 'Of course I won't send you to the boys' home!' And I'm thinking, *Did Miss Barker say she'd send him to the boys' home if he didn't have sex with her?* So I ask him, and sure enough that's

189

what she threatened him with. Okay, I threatened him yesterday with a juvenile detention centre, but that was pretty obviously a joke. Also, I was not doing it as a way of forcing him to have sex with me.

So, I think triumphantly, *Miss Barker was definitely* not *the walking, talking, living angel that everybody here thinks she was.*

And yet she has the nerve to criticise my teaching!

Anyway, so now he's saying, 'I was just trying to help her have a baby!' Sheesh, I think, she must have been desperate. I give him a hug and say, 'Listen, Ryan, yes, it was nice of you to try to help Miss Barker, but what she did to you was wrong, very wrong.' And he's blubbering something else now, and because he has his head stuck in my chest, it's all muffled but I definitely heard the word 'fiancé'. And immediately my ears prick up. I think, *Fiancé?*

Gregory?

Was Gregory her actual fiancé?

Seriously?

Would this account for his strange behaviour at the Pondage the other day? Is vomiting, groaning, ripping hand off etc. perhaps unusual expression of grief?

So now Ryan looks up at me and in this sad little voice, he says, 'Miss?'

And I'm like, 'What?'

'Could we cuddle at least?'

And I'm like, 'Well, we are sort of cuddling, aren't we?'

And he says, 'No, I mean could we cuddle on the bed?'

So I say, 'Not on the bed, Ryan.'

And he's like, 'Please? Miss Barker used to cuddle me on the bed.' And I'm like, 'I am definitely not going to cuddle you on the bed, Ryan,' because I can see where this is going and I really need to lay down some ground rules with this kid. So he says, 'What about the couch?'

Long story short, I agree to cuddle on the couch. Admittedly this is not a wise decision. There are Education Department guidelines on the subject.

It's awkward, to say the least. I sit very upright, with my arms placed gingerly around him, but then he gets frustrated that I'm not hugging him tightly enough so he flings his arms around me and I suddenly realise this kid is immensely strong, stronger than you'd think, because his arms around me are really tight, uncomfortably so, almost crushing me. And meanwhile he keeps leaning his entire body weight against me, almost as if he's trying to push me into a more horizontal position. But then the oven timer goes off, and I'm like, 'Right! Let's get those cupcakes out!' I try to struggle out of his grip but I'm actually having a huge amount of trouble extricating myself. And then I realise he has actually got himself into a position where his crotch is pressed against my leg and he is starting to literally hump me like a golden retriever, and I am thinking, Oh my God! and I keep saying, 'I have to get the cupcakes, Ryan!' because he's starting to pant quite heavily, and finally I manage to slither out of his grip but fall awkwardly onto the floor in doing so.

I have a horrible feeling he may have climaxed at that point.

Not sure, but maybe.

So I run into the kitchen and pull the cupcakes out of the oven. I'm in complete shock. I have never had an incident like this in my entire teaching career. I have literally no idea what to do. So, true to form when faced with a crisis, I follow my usual course of doing exactly nothing, except vaguely pretending that the bad thing didn't happen.

Anyway, he follows me into the kitchen and he says to me, 'Okay if I smoke?'

Because apparently Ryan enjoys a post-coital cigarette. So I put my foot down, and I say to him, 'If you are going to smoke, you have to smoke outside.'

Which again is all wrong. As his teacher, I should not be condoning smoking, post-coital or otherwise.

So he goes outside for a cigarette. And I think to myself, You know what? I could do with a ciggie myself. Not that I should smoke, of course. I'm the last person who should be smoking, what with Dad dying of lung cancer. But nevertheless I go outside and sit on the back step with Ryan, smoking his cigarettes while he tells me all about Minecraft in excruciating detail. I just nod every now and then like I give a shit, and smoke about six ciggies in a row. He doesn't care—he's just happy because he humped me. Finally, I start yawning and saying, 'Oh my gosh, look how late it is and school tomorrow.' And in fact, it is late, it's almost midnight. So I pack him off home with the cupcakes in a Tupperware container, waving goodbye from the doorstep till he disappears into the darkness.

Then I run into my bedroom, grab my suitcase and drag it out the front door and into the car. Clothes keep falling out because I haven't managed to get the zipper done up properly, but I don't care. I don't even bother picking them up. I feel like I haven't got a moment to lose. It seems absolutely imperative, particularly after the humping, that I leave town immediately. Nothing good can come of this, I feel sure.

So after a little bit of a panic when I can't find my keys but then discover them eventually fallen behind the microwave, I jump in the car and—guess what?—it won't start. It's been a bit unreliable lately; I'm thinking it needs a new battery. Anyway, I sit in the driveway, cranking and cranking the ignition until finally it won't crank anymore. I think maybe I've flooded the engine, so I sit there in the darkness for a little while, waiting for it to unflood, which is what Dad always told me to do.

And while I'm sitting there, I start thinking about my dad. I guess that's because it used to be his car, this little Corolla—I inherited it, so to speak. Well, I needed a car, so when he died I just claimed it. I find it sort of comforting, even though it's a bit of a shitbox, mainly because I don't look after it. I feel a bit ashamed about that. But anyway, there are things about it which remind me of him. The faded grey terry-towelling car seat covers, for example, almost worn through—he put those on to protect the seats. His street directory, circa 1993. The St Christopher medallion blue-tacked to the dash—not that my father was even particularly religious; I think one of his students from the Philippines gave it to him. *Behold Saint Christopher*, it says, *And Go Your Way In Safety*.

So I'm sitting there, thinking about my dad, and what a good, decent, humble, unassuming man he was, and how well he conducted himself in life and how brave and kind and thoughtful he was right up to his death. And I wonder

194

what he'd think about the way I've turned out. If he could look down from his motel heaven and see me right now.

Somehow, that's a very sobering, perspective-shifting thought.

And as I sit there in the darkness, I almost begin to feel like he is sitting there beside me in the passenger seat, the way he used to do when he was giving me driving lessons. He was the only one who could give me driving lessons—if Mum tried, we'd end up screaming at each other. Dad was calmer—he didn't fuss. If I sideswiped a parked car, he'd just say, 'Stay a little wider next time.' We'd go for long driving trips around the suburbs, maybe stopping for a milkshake as a treat. We didn't talk that much, but it never felt awkward, it just felt sort of quietly companionable. And that's how it feels now, as I'm waiting for the car to unflood. Like I'm sitting in companionable communion with my father. So eventually I say to him, 'What do you reckon, Dad?'

And he gives me that look he used to give me, that look that seemed to say that he'd hoped for better from me.

Next thing I know, I'm dragging my suitcase back inside again.

Today the grief counsellor came to talk to the children.

Her name is Mrs Moran, and from the wary way she regarded me when I introduced myself, I could see that Glenda had already fully briefed her. 'You just take a seat,' she said to me with a note of warning in her voice, like she didn't want me causing any trouble. 'I'll lead the children through this.'

So I am decommissioned to the back of the room like a failed but still dangerous nuclear reactor while she essentially takes over my classroom. Her idea of grief counselling is to get the kids to yell out anything they can think of to describe Miss Barker, while she writes their comments up on the board in fun-coloured markers. Of course, the kids think this is brilliant. Hands shooting up eagerly all over the place. Bright little animated faces.

'Caring!' someone calls out.

'Kind to animals!'

'Beautiful!'

'Gentle!'

'Understanding!'

'Good with cuddles!'

'Great stuff, keep it coming!' cries Mrs Moran.

'Creative!'

'Funny!'

'Sexy!' This from Ryan.

I snort out loud. Mrs Moran throws me a look.

'Ryan, I'm not sure that's the sort of describing word we're looking for,' she says.

So Ryan tries again. 'Sensual?'

I am impressed with his vocab. Up till now, I'd thought his literacy skills were minimal.

'I think you mean "sensitive",' says Mrs Moran, briskly writing 'sensitive' on the board. I know what he meant though. He meant what he said the first time. Sexy. Sexy, as in Miss

197

Barker liked to have sex with minors, specifically Ryan. If only they knew, I think with gritted teeth. Frankly, I am finding it all a bit galling being forced to sit and listen to my flawed predecessor being described in such rapturous terms. And as I sit there, I start to ponder random thoughts. Why was Miss Barker so desperate to get pregnant? Did Gregory want her to get pregnant? Could Gregory possibly have been her fiancé? And thinking about all this, about Gregory and Miss Barker and babies, actually starts to make me feel sick to my stomach. Like seriously nauseous.

Now Mrs Moran is talking about what song they could sing at the memorial service on Wednesday. The children suggest 'Over In The Meadow', which was Miss Barker's favourite song apparently.

'Oh, how lovely!' cries Mrs Moran, clapping her hands together while a surge of bile rises up my gullet. 'Now tell me, what was Miss Barker's favourite colour?'

Every little hand shoots up in response. 'Yellow!' they cry.

'What a lovely happy colour,' says Mrs Moran. 'I have an idea. Why don't we all wear something yellow to her funeral, as a way of celebrating what a lovely, happy person she was!'

The kids are just about demented with excitement at this idea, but it's little Rose who offers up the clincher.

'What if everyone gets a yellow balloon, and after the service, everyone lets a balloon go up in the sky?' she cries. And suddenly I realise that I am going to throw up.

'Rose, what a beautiful idea,' says Mrs Moran as I bolt from the room, my hand over my mouth. 'And what a wonderful way of expressing our feelings for Miss Barker!'

I throw up in the toilet, to the accompaniment of the children singing 'Over In The Meadow'. Luckily it goes for about twenty-nine verses, so it covers the sound of my extended retching. And as I'm leaning over the toilet bowl, hacking up every last bit of bile in my gut, a thought occurs to me.

Could I be pregnant?

Could I actually possibly be pregnant?

Could Gregory have impregnated me?

It's entirely possible. We had sex multiple times. I was ovulating (at least he seemed to think I was ovulating, since he was unable to overcome his biological impulses). And, also, I appear to have morning sickness???

And suddenly, as I'm wiping my mouth with a clump of toilet paper, I am overcome with an enormous sense of personal triumph. Personal triumph is not a sensation I am overly familiar with, but now I feel elated. This will knock Josh's nose out of joint—let's see how he likes being on the receiving end of news like this. And perhaps if I Instagram a pic which shows just how incredibly good-looking Gregory is. He is about fifty billion times better looking than Josh, that's for sure. Take that, Delores! Ha! And you too, Miss Barker.

I wash my face and I hurry back into the classroom—it's empty, because in all that time I was vomiting in the toilet, it somehow became lunchtime. (I seem to be losing track of time—is that a pregnancy thing? Possibly the hormones do something, make you vaguer or something? I think I've read that somewhere.) I run out into the playground, pull Ryan aside and ask if Gregory is in town. 'No,' says Ryan. 'He's gone away for work.' And I'm like, 'Okay, but when is he due back?' Ryan doesn't know, he just shrugs and seems very sour about things. But I refuse to let his mood bring me down—this happens too often with me. I am too subject to other people imposing their stuff on me. Like Glenda, for example.

I find her and Mrs Moran muttering about me in the kitchenette. 'Where have you been all this time?' she asks me. 'I've been in the toilet, vomiting,' I tell her cheerfully. I can't seem to wipe the grin off my face, and then I start giggling because I suddenly think how funny it would be if our baby was actually conceived on Glenda's desk. (I can't wait to tell her that at some opportune moment—imagine her face!) 'You know what?' says Mrs Moran. 'I think perhaps you should take the rest of the afternoon off. The last thing we need is gastro going through the school, especially at a time like this.' And I'm thinking, actually, what I've got ain't catching, but fine, I'll take an early mark.

It's a nice sunny day, so as I waltz out of the school grounds, I think maybe I can drive into Tumut and get a pregnancy test, and also another box of sav blanc while I'm about it. But of course, I've forgotten my car won't start, although I spend a solid twenty minutes attempting to start it anyway. So I think, well, maybe Janelle carries pregnancy tests at the shop? Of course, I wouldn't want to start gossip by actually asking Janelle straight out if she stocks pregnancy tests, but maybe I could invent a story or perhaps simply shoplift one?

I go into the shop and, sure enough, there's Janelle, and she looks at me all judgey as usual, like *why aren't you in school?* I explain that I have gastro, although this is undermined slightly by the fact that I am buying three bottles of wine. All the while I'm peering past her to the special 'pharmacy' section behind the counter, but all I can see is Nurofen and antacid and cough medicine. So no luck there.

And then, as I'm walking home, I remember my mum telling me about a homespun pregnancy test that she'd done when she was pregnant with me, and basically it involved urinating on a few dandelion leaves. But where the hell am I going to find dandelion leaves? Do I actually have any idea what dandelion leaves look like? No, I do not. I am not known for my love of Nature.

I need to get the car started so I can drive up to the Ridge and try to google dandelion leaves on my phone, so I run down to the service station and I'm like, 'Can you please come up to my house and jump-start my car for me?'

There's this nice young mechanic there, and had I met this guy before Gregory came a-knocking, I would have been spending all my time dreaming up problems with my car, because this guy is actually kind of cute, in a goofy too-tall sort of way. And he's like, 'Sure, I'll jump-start your car, but if you like I could actually fix it, seeing how that's what I do for a living.' And I'm like, 'That'd be great, but I'm actually in kind of a hurry right now.' And he's like, 'Okay, I'll get my ute.' And he brings his ute around from out the back and says, 'Hop in,' and we drive back up to my house.

Can I just say how nice it felt to sit in a normal, healthy, sane person's car for the seventy-five seconds it took to get to my place? It was heaven. He's cracking jokes and offering me gum and actually kind of flirting with me. I think to myself, Well, maybe if I am not pregnant with Gregory's demon love child, I will try to get together with this guy. But at the moment, I'm really just focused on the pregnancy.

While he's connecting the leads, I'm like, 'You don't happen to know what a dandelion looks like, do you?' And he grins and says, 'I'm guessing you're not a country girl,' and I'm like, 'No, actually,' and he leans down and picks a dandelion about one inch away from my foot. And he presents it to me like it's a rose and he's the Bachelor, dandelion spores blowing in the breeze. I'm like, 'Great! Now I don't need my car jump-started!', and he's like, 'I'll do it for you anyway, no charge,' which he does, and then he says, 'If I were you, I'd drive it round for an hour or so to charge up the battery.' And I'm thinking, Okay, well, I'll drive up to the Ridge. Because although I now have dandelion leaves, I can't actually remember what's supposed to happen when you pee on them. I mean if you're pregnant. So no choice but to call Mum and try to find out in a roundabout way, which I know in advance is a bad idea because of course she will see right through me.

So I drive up to the Ridge and perch on my usual rock, and wave my phone about in the air trying to get some reception going. As anticipated, phone call to Mum does not go well. We end up screaming at each other, surprise surprise. She does not buy my story about my 'friend' who thinks she might be pregnant, and gets very snappy and says, 'Stop lying to me, Eleanor, I am not an idiot!' Then she gets it into her head that me being pregnant is just the worst possible thing given my breast cancer, because according to my mother, who is a self-appointed Professor of Breast Cancer and avid reader of online forums on the subject, my sort of cancer feeds on oestrogen or whatever the pregnancy hormone is, so basically I tell her that I am placing a ban on any further communication with her for three months. I do these bans periodically. I have done ever since I was about twelve.

I mean, I thought she always wanted grandchildren! Seriously, you can't win with her sometimes.

Anyway, I get back into the car and it almost doesn't start again because of course I only drove it for about ten minutes as opposed to the 'hour or so' that my lovely mechanic recommended. But, thank God, it does finally kick over so I drive home at speed, jump out of the car, run into the house and grab a plastic container, because basically I am busting to pee and I need to pee all over these dandelion leaves.

Okay, so what follows is a tad on the weird side. I sit there on the toilet staring at my plastic container of yellow piss and dandelion leaves, swishing them round from time to time in a bid to speed up the process. For the longest time nothing happens. I start to feel myself sinking into the abyss all over again. I begin to berate myself for getting my hopes up and allowing myself to get all carried away on this slim, meagre, hopeless possibility. Berating myself doesn't seem enough punishment though, so I begin to punch myself hard on my thighs and arms until I mottle and bruise, but even this doesn't satisfy me. Finally, I stand up and put my fist through the flimsy, mouldering gyprock of the toilet wall. That feels better. And I'm just about to flush the urine and dandelion potion down the toilet when suddenly I notice something. Strange dark purplish spots, barely perceptible at first, are beginning to appear on the dandelion leaves. Then, before my fascinated gaze, they start to swell up and blister. It's disgusting. I'm thinking, what kind of fiendish hormone is this that causes these hideous festering ulcers on this sweet innocent little dandelion plant?

A pregnancy hormone, that's what!! Hooray!!!!

Just trying to have a quiet moment to reflect and gather my thoughts.

I'm expecting a baby.

Even writing down the words feels momentous.

But you know what? Things really need to change around here. I need to get my act together. No more nonsense. Time to behave like a grown-up.

Should I tell Gregory? I think it's only fair. He has a right to know. Plus I have a hunch he's going to be super excited about it. Maybe shocked at first. Like, it might take a bit of getting used to. But I know for a fact that he's going to be an amazing Dad. Strict possibly, like he is with Ryan, but that's okay, I can be the fun lenient one. I'll be like, 'Go ask your father.' And Gregory will be like, 'Go ask your mother.' Possibly we'll argue sometimes about child-rearing things, but that's normal. Most couples don't see completely eye to eye. Like, I could easily imagine Gregory being the total maniac tennis coach Dad. Hours of practice on the courts, screaming at the kid if he drops a point, that sort of thing. Beatings, possibly, with a tennis racquet. But you know what? Compared with what a lackadaisical slack-arse I am, maybe a little bit of that's not such a bad thing.

- - - - - - - - - - - - - - - - - - - -

More and more I have the feeling that if I can only set down events in a straightforward chronological orderly fashion then perhaps I can make sense of these things that are happening to me one after another and maybe hold on to my sanity. Because I am feeling very confused, very bewildered, very shaken up all the time. This can't be healthy. This can't be good for my breast cancer.

First there's the memorial service—that is, the memorial service for Miss Barker. The Praying Mantis leering at us through his wine-blackened teeth. The children singing 'Over In The Meadow', all dressed in yellow, their little faces tear-stained and earnest. Me conducting, or at least waving my arms about. Miss Barker's parents in the front pew, quietly dignified in their grief. (How short they are! Why are old people so short?) Next to them—this is where it gets interesting—a figure all hunched over, weeping and wailing like Oscar Pistorius. The fiancé, I'm thinking, it has to be. So I'm sneaking furtive glances, but it's impossible to get a good look at him. I can see that there is something very weird about his hair, however. It's bright gold, curly, synthetic, like a fancy-dress wig from a two-dollar shop.

The song drones on and on, verse after monotonous verse. I mean, there are actually only ten verses, but about halfway through you enter into a state of suspended consciousness, like seriously you start using less oxygen, your heart rate practically stops, there's no discernible brain activity. So anyway, we're up to the verse about the old mother frog and her little froggies seven when suddenly I notice Ryan materialising at the back of the church. I hadn't even registered up to that point that he was missing. He's wearing a yellow T-shirt as per the dress code, but even from here I can see that he's sopping wet and covered in mud. He seems very intent, very purposeful, and as he marches down the aisle, his sandshoes squelching with every step, I see that he's holding very carefully in both hands the Tupperware container I gave him the other night. I'm thinking, What has he got in that container? Surely not cupcakes? Why is he bringing cupcakes into the church? And as he gets closer, I can see what looks like reeds, dirty brown water, some indistinct shape floating inside of it, and I think, *Shit! He's found the hand! He's found Miss Barker's hand!*

So I panic. I'm thinking that Ryan's going to make a scene here, an unpleasant scene involving the grisly hand, and it is imperative that I somehow head him off. I break away from my conducting (the song still droning on and on) and I move up the aisle towards him. I'm going, 'Ryan! Ryan!

What are you doing?' But he pays me no attention and just tries to move past me. So now I realise that I have to act. I grab hold of him as forcefully as I can, basically making a citizen's arrest. He resists. We start wrestling violently in the middle of the church. He's screaming, *'Let go of me! You're hurting me! Let go of me!'*, and now I'm vaguely aware that people are standing up and shouting at me. One of the dads is trying to pull me off. All the while I'm trying to wrench the Tupperware container out of Ryan's grasp and he's struggling like a maniac, and in the midst of all this commotion, Miss Barker's semi-putrefied hand, still clutching the clump of stalks, falls out of the container and onto the carpet.

This next bit I can barely bring myself to think about.

Okay, so the impact of the drop causes the stalks to fall free of its grasp. For a moment the hand just lies there, a hideous slimy thing, much of its flesh rotted away, its thin little chicken bones exposed. A couple of fingernails remain, and I realise with a jolt that Miss Barker wore the same Revlon Posh Pink nail polish that I do. So I'm staring down at the repulsive thing when, I swear to God, before my eyes, *the fingers begin to unfurl.* I cannot believe what I'm seeing, I mean I'm literally flabbergasted. The fingers wiggle about in the air for a moment, and I actually laugh out loud because it's comical, it's like a beetle on its back except it's not, it's Miss Barker's putrid rotting appendage. But I guess my amusement must have made it angry, because suddenly it heaves itself over so the palm is facing downwards on the ecclesiastical carpet. It lies there inert for a moment, as if resting, but then very cautiously the fingers begin a kind of creeping motion, uncertain at first but gathering confidence. Now *the ghastly hand is starting to propel itself along the carpet*! At first it sets off gamely towards the back of the church and then suddenly it stops. It seems confused. It wiggles two fingers about like antennae and apparently gets a whiff of something because it suddenly executes a very decisive one-eighty so now it is facing towards me. I scream, but my scream seems to galvanise the little fucker and it sets off down the aisle towards me, scuttling, almost crab-like; you'd be surprised how fast it could move. So I'm screaming and trying to get out of its way, but the more I retreat, the more hell-bent it seems on pursuing me, and somehow I can't seem to retreat any further because someone has my elbows pinned behind my back, and now the hand has reached the toe of my shoe. It hesitates a moment, raises a couple of fingers in the air, and then—sweet Jesus—it launches itself onto my shoe and digs its few remaining talons into the soft flesh of my ankles.

Then there is a blank (I'm having a lot of blanks). I don't know what happened. Maybe I fainted.

The next thing I know, I find myself hunched over a toilet, and I'm throwing up. I feel like maybe I've been throwing up for a while because my throat is red raw, and yet I have absolutely no memory of how long I've been here. Can you throw up when you're unconscious? I guess so—drunks do it all the time. I become aware of voices outside my cubicle, women's voices talking in hushed tones, and now as I rest my cheek against the toilet seat I try to hear what they're saying, but I can't quite make anything out. The toilet seat feels cool against my skin, and that's nice because I feel hot, extremely hot, probably feverish. Someone knocks on the door to ask me if I'm all right. I wipe my mouth on the sleeve of my blouse and I get up and flush the toilet and stagger out. And there's Glenda and Mrs Moran standing by the basins, staring at me. They are 'gravely concerned', says Mrs Moran. Apparently I took a turn. I made a terrible scene in the church. And I say, 'But the hand! You saw the hand!' And they say, 'What hand? What are you talking about?' And I say, 'Miss Barker's hand! The hand that Ryan brought in!' And they say, 'Ryan brought the turtle in, Tommy the turtle, because of the song. *An old mother turtle and her little turtle one.* It was Tommy that fell out of the Tupperware container. We all thought the shock had killed him because at first he didn't move, but then, one by one, his little legs came out and off he went, marching down the carpet.'

And now Friar Hernandez pokes his head into the bathroom. And he says, 'How is she? Is she all right?' And Glenda says, 'She's not well, not well at all,' shaking her head and pretending to be all concerned about my welfare. And Friar Hernandez says, 'Ladies, may I have a moment in private with her, please?' And I'm thinking, *No, please, please, no moment in private with Friar Hernandez.* But the two women obediently scurry out and leave me alone with him.

So now he leans against the wash-basins and folds his arms, and surveys me very seriously, very intently. I know he's up to something so I decide to get on the front foot.

'How's your prostate?' I ask, all innocent.

He raises his eyebrows in surprise.

'Much better, thank you for asking,' he replies. He seems taken aback, touched even, by my concern. 'I'm on a strict regimen of prayer and fasting, also tiny radioactive pellets have been inserted in my scrotum. There's some bruising and tenderness admittedly, and bicycling must be avoided in the short-term, but otherwise, prognosis-wise, I have reason to be optimistic.'

'Well,' I say, rolling my eyes elaborately to indicate sarcasm. 'I'm glad to hear it. Especially after the performance you bunged on in the classroom the other day.'

'Ah,' he says, and his face hardens. 'That's more like it. That's more what I've come to expect.'

And then he says, 'I'm going to ask you a simple question, Eleanor.'

I'm thinking, Here we go.

Then he asks me if I've had any visitors.

And I'm like (frowning), '*Visitors?* Are you asking me if I've *ever* had any visitors? Like, in my entire life? Or just if I've had any visitors lately?' I'm being all pedantic because I'm trying to stall him, I'm trying to buy time. But he's not going to brook any nonsense from me, so he says, very slowly and deliberately, 'I'm asking you if you've had any visitors *lately*. And by *lately*, I mean specifically since the exorcism I performed on you.'

So I say, 'As a matter of fact, no. No, I haven't received any visitors since that totally unwarranted and unasked-for pagan ritual you put me through.'

Which was a lie, of course. Because I have had a visitor. In fact, I've had several visitors, but specifically I'm thinking of the visitor of all visitors, the incredibly beautiful golden-skinned taut-torsoed Gregory, tippy-toeing around my house like he's casing the place.

And he says, 'Are you sure? Cast your mind back. Bear in mind, they can be masters of disguise.'

And I make a big show of casting my mind back, and then I say, 'Nope. Pretty sure no visitors.'

He sighs very heavily. And then he's off, spouting the Bible at me: '*The unclean spirit when he is cast out of man passes through arid places, seeking rest blah blah; and finding none, he sayeth, I will turn back unto my house from whence I came. And he taketh seven other spirits more evil than himself, and they enter in and blah-de-blah-blah till the last state of the man becometh worse than the first.'*

Something like that anyway. I don't know what it is, but anytime anyone starts rabbiting on with Bible quotes, I pretty much tune out completely. Basically I just stand there and wait for his mouth to stop flapping. And when it does finally stop flapping, I'm like, 'Um, did you say something just then?'

He's getting exasperated with me now. He shifts his bony arse on the wash-basin and cocks his head to one side, regarding me in a way that I guess he hopes looks 'quizzical'.

'All right,' he says. 'In plain English. When the demon is cast out, it comes back—do you understand?—only seven times worse than before.'

And then he says, 'In cancer terms, if you like, you could say it *metastasises.*'

I can't think of a comeback because the wooziness returns to me now. I'm feeling overheated, not quite comprehending. All I know is I don't like that word 'metastasises'. I've never liked the word, and I particularly don't like the word coming from Friar Hernandez. If anyone is going to talk to me about metastases, let it be Doc, my dear beloved Doc with his bald patch and his kind eyes and his warm hands. Not this creep, not the Praying Mantis.

But now he leans in horribly close so I can smell his rancid communion wine breath: *'Seven other spirits more evil than the first. And you, stupid girl, keep inviting them in!'*

And suddenly he reels back and slaps me hard across the face. So hard I'm thrown against the toilet doors and then I ricochet into the hand dryer, setting it off. I drop down on all fours, totally in shock, staring at his trouser legs. I literally cannot believe what is happening to me. Next thing—I don't even stop to think—I've got my jaws clamped tight around his bony trousered shins. I'm sinking my teeth in hard and it feels good, it feels really good. I suddenly think, *This is why dogs like postmen!* and even through the polyester/viscose, I'm beginning to taste the sweet saltiness of his blood. He's screaming and shaking his leg and trying to pull me off by the scruff of my neck, but that just makes me dig in deeper, jerking my head from side to side to toss him around a bit. He doesn't seem to enjoy that much at all.

Finally, I take pity on his whimpering and release him. I escape out the bathroom door and find myself in the sunshine, so bright and yellow it makes me flinch. I duck into the shade behind a tree, and after a minute or two my eyes adjust and I begin to make sense of what I'm looking at. The entire congregation is assembled outside, each holding a yellow balloon. People seem to be giving speeches. Now Mrs Moran passes the microphone to Ryan and he reads aloud from a piece of paper.

'If roses grow in heaven
Lord, please pick a bunch for me
Place them in Miss Barker's arms
And tell her they're from me.'

Bad timing, I know, but I immediately throw up.

Mainly just bile and bits of flesh and small fragments of
Friar Hernandez's trousers. No one pays me much attention
because they're all releasing the balloons which are floating
skywards and everybody *oohs* and *ahhs* and claps their hands
like they've never seen a balloon before. But I've got my eye
on the fiancé in his strange wig. He's standing between Miss
Barker's oldies with an arm around each of them, and they're
gazing up at the yellow balloons as they disappear into the
heavens and poor old Mr Barker is wiping away a tear. I start
circling around through the crowd towards them, because
I'm determined to get a good look at this fiancé guy, this
supposed betrothed of Miss Barker. I need to know if it's
Gregory lurking under that wig.

And as I'm edging closer, he suddenly turns and looks straight
at me. It's like he knew I was coming, like he sensed it, and I
get a jolt, like a cold chill, because of course it *is* Gregory. It's
most definitely Gregory, even though for some reason he is
wearing this ludicrous wig. And as our eyes lock, his finger
rises fleetingly to his lips as if urging me to be quiet. Then
he turns away and allows himself to be pulled into a warm
embrace by Miss Barker's mother.

But I'm not about to keep quiet. Not after what I've been through. So I go marching up to him, and I tap him on the shoulder. And when he turns, I say, '*Why didn't you tell me you were her fiancé?*'

I'm actually startled by how different my voice sounds. Perhaps it's damaged from all the vomiting, but it's deeper and scratchier, and the sound of it shocks me, and it seems to shock everyone around me. But Gregory just looks at me blankly. 'I'm sorry?' he says. Quite politely, like he has no idea who I am. So I grab hold of his arm, and in my scary new voice, I say, '*I'm having your baby, you bastard.*'

Not quite how I pictured breaking the news.

And yet it seems to have an effect.

I see a flash of something pass over his face. It's so fleeting I have difficulty identifying the emotion he's revealing, but I sense that it's positive, so I'm momentarily extremely encouraged. It's like for a split second I see a future for us, and it's Gregory running through a house with a chubby, chortling baby on his shoulders and me laughing and calling out, 'Mind the door frame!'

But this brief hopeful vision evaporates almost instantaneously, because he turns to the Barkers and says, 'I'm sorry. I have no idea who she is or what she's talking about.'

So I lunge at him. Specifically, I lunge at his wig, because I'm keen to expose his true identity, but he's quick, and he dodges me. I try again, but he ducks behind Mr and Mrs Barker, poking his head up between them like a jack-in-the-box. And they're all bewildered and confused, and Mrs Barker is flailing at me with her handbag, and Gregory is meanwhile grinning at me from behind them. So I try again, faster this time because I'm getting angry, but at that exact same moment, Mr Barker moves across in an attempt to deflect me, and I slam my closed fist into the side of his skull, skittling him. I mean, he literally spins like a top and face-plants into the gravel. It's terrible.

Again, another big blank around here. A memory lapse, a blackout of some kind. Mercifully perhaps.

Next thing—how did I get here?—I'm in the classroom at school, and it seems I'm being interrogated by various senior figures from the Education Department, here to pay tribute to one of their own. I only know this because I ask them, 'Who are you again?' They tell me who they are, and I'm like, 'Why are you here?' And they explain that they have travelled here for Miss Barker's memorial service, but I still feel really confused. 'But what's that got to do with me?' I keep asking. I feel if I ask a lot of questions it will somehow give me the upper hand. Too often I take the passive route. I just lie back and let bad things happen to me. This has got to stop if I want to get anywhere in life.

'Well, we're extremely concerned about you,' says a man with strikingly circular glasses. This is where I'm headed if I keep teaching, I think. Statement eyewear. 'I suppose we're wondering,' he continues, 'if you didn't go back to work too soon—after your illness, I mean. Because some of the parents have spoken to us, and they're not very happy. Apparently you never mark anything; you never plan any outcomes. There have been reports of you swearing at the children. Also, there's the rough way you dealt with Ryan today. Surely you're aware of the guidelines concerning physical contact with students?'

I nod vaguely. I've become distracted by the sight of Tommy, lurking innocently in his tank. Ha! I think bitterly. Am I somehow supposed to believe that that turtle's been to church today? Good try, ladies.

'Look,' says Statement Eyewear's colleague, the fat one. She chooses to express her individuality in bold geometric patterns, like camouflage on a warship. 'We understand that it's a very difficult thing, stepping into the shoes of a teacher as exceptional and as loved as Miss Barker ... '

'Oh, Miss Barker!' I cry in my scary new voice. 'Miss Barker, Miss Barker, Miss Barker! I'm sick to death of hearing about her. And btw, fyi, perhaps your Miss Barker wasn't quite as wonderful as you think she was. I could tell you some stories about your Miss B that would curl your hair.'

'*How dare you!*' cries Glenda, rising from her seat at the back of the room. 'How dare you cast aspersions on Miss Barker when she's not here to defend herself. Well, let me tell you this, young lady—you're not half the teacher she was, and nor will you ever be blah blah ... '

I guess she went on in that vein. I can't really remember. Again, I must have blanked out. Some small part of my brain seems to be shutting down. I'm sitting here and I'm trying to remember, but there are just these great gaping blanks all the way through, like there are literally giant holes in the webbing of my brain, I can picture it. I know that at some point through her tirade, I became aware of a heaviness in the pit of my belly and a warm seeping feeling in my undies. I guess that was when I started to cry, because I realised then that I must be bleeding, that I had my period, which of course meant I wasn't pregnant after all—so much for the stupid dandelion leaves. Or maybe I was pregnant for about a minute, and now I was having a miscarriage. Either way, I was feeling pretty crushingly disappointed, and the last thing I needed at that moment was Glenda haranguing me. Because me being pregnant with Gregory's baby was probably the one thin thread that was holding me together, my one sense of purpose and achievement. All gone. All washed away in the mucousy red fluid that was currently soiling my undies, and the back of my skirt, and also the green vinyl seat of the chair I was sitting on. So apart from me sitting there and bleeding and weeping, I have no real idea how that meeting ended. My guess is, taking Glenda's lead, they all joined in giving me a well-deserved dressing down. Maybe they even sacked me, who knows?

I suppose I have to pause here and take stock and ask myself the tough question: is it my fault that these bad things keep happening? Have I brought all this upon myself, with my bad attitude and my negativity and my weakness of character? In all honesty, if I am being totally candid, I would have to admit that the answer to that question is 'possibly'. It's not like I haven't had problems before in the workplace. I've definitely noticed that sometimes people don't like me, by which I mean they take a dislike to me for random unknown reasons—often before I've actually even done anything to earn their dislike. Case in point: Glenda. But on the other hand, and it's well-documented in the annals of my work history, I am by nature very quick to fly off the handle. What I did to Friar Hernandez, for example. That was maybe a bit of an overreaction on my part. Honestly, when I think back, it looked like a shark had attacked him. I even thought for a moment that maybe I should apply some kind of tourniquet, but there was nothing really suitable to use and also I actually have no idea how to apply a tourniquet so I just left him. Anyway, I can't think about that right now.

The next thing I remember is I'm staggering home and I'm sobbing so hard I can barely see where I'm going. The reason I am sobbing, of course, is because I am bleeding, quite copiously, which I shouldn't be, because I should be pregnant. So I guess what I'm experiencing is disappointment. Crushing disappointment combined with sheer disbelief and a sense of the absolute unfairness of it all. At some point amid the sobbing and the staggering, I realise that Daphne, the incredible shrunken woman, has fallen into step beside me. I have no idea she's even there until she takes one of those mini-packs of tissues from her handbag and gives it to me. I'm super surprised. I'm also touched by the gesture so I thank her, and as I'm pulling out a tissue she says, in her nervy little voice, 'Time to go.'

What? I'm blowing my nose at this point, but I pause mid-blow to look at her.

'It's time to leave,' she says. 'You can catch the bus.'

'Bus?'

'There's a bus on Thursday.'

'What day is it today?' I ask. 'I'm losing track.'

'There's a bus on Thursday for those afflicted,' says Daphne.

I stare at her. I'm wondering if I've heard her correctly, but perhaps my expression seems somehow sneering and derisive. Because now, like I've offended her, she veers off abruptly, crossing over the road. A wave of irritation washes over me, not for the first time today.

'Afflicted with what, Daphne?' I call after her. *'With what am I afflicted?'*

But she pays me no attention, she just keeps going.

I stand there on the corner, exhausted. Just physically and emotionally drained—not surprising really, given the day I've had. I find myself staring at the street sign—it's bent at an angle, like something big has scraped against it. It seems significant somehow, but I can't think why.

So imagine my surprise when I walk in the front door and find Ryan sitting on my couch. In some ways, he's the last person I want to see, but at the same time I'm glad of some company.

'Ryan,' I say, sitting down beside him, 'I'm really sorry if I handled you roughly. Did I hurt you?'

'Just a bruise,' he says. But he shows me his forearm, and there's a great mass of horrible purple welts up and down it, like I've given him sixteen Chinese burns.

'Oh God,' I say. 'I seriously do not know my own strength. You see, I thought that you had somehow found Miss Barker's hand, and you were bringing it into church.'

'It was just Tommy!' says Ryan, smiling up at me. 'Why would I bring Miss Barker's hand into church?'

'I know, it's silly,' I say. 'But that's what I thought, anyway. I honestly thought Miss Barker's hand was crawling after me.'

'Like she was out to get you?' asks Ryan, his eyes shining eagerly.

'Exactly,' I say. 'It's nuts, right?'

We both laugh. And you know what? It felt good to have someone to share a joke with. Someone who doesn't judge me like the rest of them. For some reason, I like this lumpy kid. I give him a jovial punch in the arm, but for some reason he stops laughing now.

'Maybe she *was* out to get you,' says Ryan. 'Maybe she's angry.'

Here we go again. Miss Barker and her unsolicited performance reviews.

'Angry?' I say wearily. 'Why would Miss Barker be angry?'

'She's angry about what happened to her. Also, she's jealous. She's jealous of you and him.'

Uh-oh. This is the first time we've ever touched upon this delicate subject. By which I mean the subject of Gregory, Ryan's brother—Miss Barker's fiancé in the fancy-dress wig.

'She knows about me and Gregory?' I ask.

'Of course she knows. And another thing,' he continues, 'she's jealous of you and me.'

'But there's nothing between you and me!' I cry, although suddenly, in the moment, I don't feel a hundred per cent sure about this. I'm trying to remember if something did actually happen between Ryan and me. I can vaguely recall some kind of incident on the couch, the same couch we're sitting on now.

'I'm just saying,' says Ryan, 'if she was alive, she would probably be jealous. But she's dead, so she's not.'

I guess around now I notice that I'm still bleeding so I go into the bathroom to try to staunch the flow, because it's like, torrential; it's practically biblical. While I'm in the bathroom, I notice the hole I punched in the wall the other day and it makes me feel sad all over again. So I punch another hole. And while I'm at it, another one.

And suddenly, in the midst of all that punching, I remember something from the breast cancer support group I went to a hundred years ago, in my previous life. Specifically, I remember this woman, a little younger than the rest, a little quieter, a little less inclined to the hugging and the laughter. When it was her turn to share, she produced from her handbag an ultrasound image of a foetus. And we're all blinking at it and thinking, Whoa, is that what we think it is? Why is she showing this to us? And she says, 'I wanted to share with you this picture of my baby boy,' and then before she gets any further, she starts to cry. And for about five solid minutes she cannot get another word out but she's very insistently gesturing that we should pass the ultrasound around even though, in all honesty, there wasn't much to look at. I mean, I'm not even sure how they managed to determine it was a boy. And then, very haltingly, she finally manages to tell us that she had to terminate this pregnancy when she found out she had cancer because she had to start treatment straight away, no mucking around. And she's saying, 'I'm sorry, I thought I was ready to talk about it, but I guess I'm not,' and now everyone else is crying too, you couldn't help it. It was the saddest, saddest thing.

It was her first pregnancy, and she even had the names picked out. He was going to be Harry Ellery Leo Parker. I always remember that because the initials spelled HELP. I don't think she realised.

I was the last one to get the ultrasound image, so I had to hand it back to her.

'He's really cute,' I said. 'He would have been a cute baby. Did you realise his initials spell "HELP"?'

She just looked at me like I was a mad person. (This was even before I brought up all the stuff about the underwire bras.) But my point is, standing there in my smashed-up bathroom, I guess I understand for the first time how she felt. Because you're either growing a baby or you're growing a tumour. You can't do both.

'Hey, Miss,' says Ryan, when eventually I come out of the bathroom. He doesn't mention the punching of walls and the wailing and stuff, though my guess is he probably heard it. 'Can you keep a secret?'

'Okay,' I say dully, sitting back down on the couch. My knuckles hurt. Also, now I look at them, they're bruised and swelling.

Ryan leans forward and whispers in my ear, 'I do have her hand. Which is why I was late this morning.'

Oh great, I think. This truly caps off the entire day.

'I found it in the Pondage,' he says proudly.

'And what exactly are you intending to do with it?' I ask.

'I dunno.' He shrugs. 'Keep it.'

I try to remember what the Education Department guidelines might have to say about a situation like this. *Dismembered Appendages*. Have I seen that on a drop-down menu on the website somewhere? It feels like maybe I have. In any case, I need to be firm with him.

'Ryan,' I say, 'you can't keep it. You have to hand it in to the police.'

And he giggles at this: '*Hand* it in!' And I'm like, 'No, stop laughing. I'm serious Ryan. You have to hand it—*you have to give the fucking hand to the police!*' I'm actually yelling at him. I'm yelling at him so loud it takes me a moment to realise there's someone banging on the front door.

Banging very loudly on the front door.

Can I say? A huge sense of foreboding overtakes me.

I look at Ryan. He's sort of stiffened. He's all watchful, wary. He looks at me. I put a finger to my lips in warning then, extremely cautiously, I approach the door.

'Who is it?' I enquire, trying to sound unsuspecting.

'Sorry to bother you,' says a voice on the other side. 'Would you be interested in purchasing a vacuum cleaner?'

I mean, for Pete's sake.

The gall of this guy.

'No thank you!' I call back, casual as anything.

Super quietly, I set about sliding the bolts across the door. Because something about what Friar Hernandez said to me has actually sunk in. The bit about me continually letting in visitors. It's true. If someone knocks, my absolute knee-jerk reaction is—guess what?—I open the door. That's how gullible and stupid and needy I am. For once I should actually say, 'Get lost!' For once I should actually say, 'You're not welcome.'

'I have a very special offer for a limited time only,' says the voice on the other side of the door.

'*Get lost!*' I shout.

You know how it feels? It feels empowering! I'm surprised at myself for having the gumption.

Okay, so now things go ominously quiet. I listen warily, my ear to the door. I look at Ryan. He's all tense, on the balls of his feet, poised to run. He cocks his head as if he's heard something and immediately I think, Oh God! The back door! And I rush towards it, but I'm too late. He's already in.

It's Gregory, of course.

Surprise, surprise.

He's taken his silly wig off but now he's holding a vacuum cleaner and a briefcase. Also, he has a look on his face. If I had to try and describe it in a court of law, I would say that his features had arranged themselves in such a way as to express his disappointment in me.

'Eleanor,' he says, 'you are not being very hospitable.'

And then Ryan emerges from the lounge room, and this seems to piss Gregory off even more.

'What are you doing here?' says Gregory.

'She invited me,' says Ryan.

'You invited him?' asks Gregory, turning to me, all affronted.

'Well, not exactly,' I say, which is true.

'Then go home, Ryan,' asks Gregory. 'Your services are not required here.'

Ryan is not very happy about this, but he skulks past us out the door. As he passes, Gregory cuffs him lightly over the head, and Ryan wheels around and absolutely decks him. I'm thinking, Attaboy! Gregory reels back against the broom cupboard, but only for a moment because then he spins around, leaps up and kicks Ryan with both feet in the chest. Well, Ryan drops like a rag doll, but Gregory just picks him up by the scruff of the neck and boots him out the back door. Then he locks it, employing all twenty-three of Miss Barker's various locks.

'He's a good kid most of the time,' he says, turning back to me. 'Puberty. You know how it is.'

Now here's the thing. Being locked in the house with Gregory made me extremely uneasy. I admit to feeling super wary of the guy. He's an oddball, a scamp, a mischief-maker. His teeth are strange. Also the way his earlobes join his head. Frankly I don't know what I ever saw in him. Besides, experience has taught me that he's inclined to behave unpredictably. So I'm edging back into the lounge room, but he just follows me with his vacuum cleaner.

'We have a special offer for the mum-to-be,' he's saying, as he plugs it into the wall socket. 'A complimentary carpet-buster deep clean—totally free and at no cost to you. It's simply that we're in the area and doing this as a word-of-mouth promotional.'

He opens his briefcase then, and produces a small wooden box, vaguely familiar, extensively decorated with decoupage. He prises off the lid with a screwdriver, and then scatters what looks like ashes all over the carpet. It takes him a while. By the time he finishes wafting it about, the carpet is inches thick with the stuff.

'Did you know that eighty per cent of waste vacuumed is actually dead skin and nose-pickings?' says Gregory. 'Disgusting, huh? You don't want Bubs crawling around in that.'

With a click of his foot, he turns the vacuum cleaner on. It's unbelievably noisy. To judge by the fact that his lips are moving, he seems to be explaining the features, but I can't hear a word of it over the din. I have to admit, though, the vacuum cleaner is pretty effective. He's making good headway hoovering up the ashes. Occasionally, when bone fragments get sucked up the nozzle, they make a nasty pinging sound and this causes him to frown and shake the nozzle a bit, but he keeps right on vacuuming nonetheless. He takes off the sweeper attachment and puts on a nozzle, and he uses this to get in all the corners and crevices. He puts on another attachment and runs this over the curtains and soft furnishings, and again it's extremely effective. Finally, the room is absolutely spotless. He clicks off the vacuum cleaner with the heel of his soft leather shoe.

'How about that?' he says, with a wave of his hand. 'Do you think your current vacuum cleaner could do this good a job?'

I have to admit it probably couldn't. To be honest, I'm not even sure I have a vacuum cleaner.

'Okay, so now we get to the exciting bit,' says Gregory. 'In light of your condition, I'm delighted to offer you a once-in-a-lifetime deal, courtesy of my employer.'

'I'm not interested,' I say. Because the whole time he's been vacuuming, I've been trying to come up with a plan. This is difficult because my brain is so scrambled and soft and jelly-like, and the best I can come up with is this: *Get him out of here.* Also, it seems terribly important all of a sudden that I not enlighten him as to the fact of my not actually being pregnant, especially after he's spent like seriously forty-five minutes vacuuming my living room. Meanwhile Gregory's pulled out a calculator and he's stabbing at numbers randomly with his forefinger.

'Okay, how about twelve monthly payments of fifty-six dollars and twenty-eight cents? How good does that sound?'

'I don't want the vacuum cleaner.'

'You can't just say, "I don't want the vacuum cleaner." You have to give me a reason.'

'I can't afford it.'

'Come on! That's less than two bucks a day. Besides, we can help with the financing.'

'Forget it.'

'I see what you're doing,' says Gregory. 'You're playing hard-ball. Okay. Let me call my boss and see what he can do.'

He then pulls out a mobile phone and speed dials. A lengthy conversation ensues in which he is apparently being berated by his boss and can hardly get a word in. There's a lot of 'But sir—' and 'With respect—' and 'I tried to explain that, but the customer claims not to be interested.' Finally, he

236

goes, 'Really? Okay. If you say so.' Then he hangs up and looks at me.

'Wow,' he says. 'Is this your lucky day or what? The boss has thought it through, and he says, Just take it. Take the vacuum cleaner. Gratis. On the house. It's yours, as a gift, with our compliments.'

'I don't want it,' I say, because I'm pretty certain it's a trick. I know for a fact there's no mobile reception here.

'Oh, come on! Are you kidding me?'

'Get out,' I say, very quietly and firmly.

He looks at me then, a strange expression on his face. I feel a stab of fear, because I remember him telling me way back on our first date that he's a really sweet, docile guy until some- one crosses him, and here I am deliberately crossing him. He begins to whistle a little tune. Very calmly, very nonchalant, he unplugs the vacuum cleaner and presses a button with his foot, and the cord whizzes noisily back inside the vacuum cleaner. That takes a while as it's a very long cord, and at one point it snakes itself around my leg and I briefly fear I'm about to be sucked up into the vacuum cleaner also, but I manage to shake it off with a bit of fancy footwork and Gregory smirks at me and says, 'Is that what you call dancing like nobody's watching?'

Arsehole.

Then he picks up his briefcase and the vacuum cleaner and he moves towards the back door. I follow him. And this is where I made my mistake. In my anxiety to carry through my plan, I allowed myself to follow him more closely (up to that point I had been trying to keep a distance), and the reason I did this was that I was planning to slam the door on him the minute he stepped outside. So I'm following maybe a foot behind him when suddenly he stops and swivels around. His nostrils twitch like a rabbit's and his eyes narrow.

'You *are* actually pregnant, aren't you?'

'Yes.'

'Okay.' His eyes have come over all glassy. 'I hope so. I'd hate to think I went through all of that for nothing.'

The minute he's gone, I slam the door behind him and slide all the bolts across, one after the other.

For a long time, I just lie on the bed.

I seem to be experiencing a variety of symptoms. My breast, for example, is twinging violently. My belly aches. My knuckles are throbbing. Strange thoughts crowd my mind, none of them comforting. I am thinking a lot about poor legless Friar Hernandez and his demons. You cast them out and they come back like gate crashers, seven times worse than before.

I feel pretty bad about chewing his leg off. In many ways, he's been the only one who's ever shown any concern for me, and how do I respond? With physical violence. I'm wondering if he's even survived. Has anybody thought to look for him? Could he still be there now, bleeding out in the ladies' toilets? Should I go see if he's there, still alive? I could take a belt as a tourniquet. Some towels maybe.

No.

I know in my heart it would be too late.

Besides, bad things happen when I venture outside.

The longer I lie here, the more certain I am that the cancer has metastasised. Can you tell? I think you can.

It's so unfair. I shouldn't even be able to spell that word.

The longer I lie here, the more certain I am that it's brain mets.

I have a strange feeling in my skull.

I think it's eating its way through my head.

The longer I lie here, the more certain I am that Gregory is some kind of demon, maybe an incubus. Possibly Ryan too. Maybe even Josh. Maybe this all goes back to Josh. That makes sense. After all, Josh made me sick in the first place.

He always insists that I broke up with him, but that was just Josh trying to make himself look less of a bastard after I went and got cancer. Let's just say that he somewhat rewrote the history books to benefit himself. The truth is that he broke up with me and he chose our four-year anniversary dinner to do it. We were having dinner at Mancini's. We had this thing (my idea) that on our anniversary we always do everything exactly the same as our first proper date—order the same food, the same wine, sit at the same table etc. But Josh is in some kind of weird mood because he goes ahead and orders the exact opposite of what he should have ordered. He should have ordered the risotto marinara, but now he says he doesn't want to order the risotto marinara—in fact he doesn't want to eat seafood at all anymore on account of the fact that there are no sustainable fisheries. So instead he orders a meat-lover's pizza. Then he insists on having red wine instead

242

of white wine, his reason being that you can't have white wine with a meat-lover's pizza. I mean, he deliberately did everything the *exact opposite*, just to fucking annoy me. So of course I sit there crying over my garlic bread because he's deliberately wrecking everything, and that's when he tells me my moods are erratic. Which is rich—I mean, who ordered the meat-lover's pizza if you want to talk about erratic? And then he goes on to tell me that he's finding our relationship *exhausting*. He wants some *emotional stability*. I'm like, Well, *who's deliberately destabilising our anniversary dinner?!* So I get up from the table and I don't come back. But just to confuse him, I leave my handbag so he thinks I've just gone to the bathroom, and he sits there eating his meat-lover's pizza and drinking his entire bottle of shiraz waiting for me to return, which I never do. And that's why he tells the world that I dumped him. But I happen to know that the whole time Delores must have been waiting in the wings because, seriously, about one week later I hear that they're dating.

Not that I truly blame Josh for giving me cancer, but the fact remains, three months later I'm scratching my armpit and bingo.

All I know about incubi is they like to fornicate with mortal women. Which proves it. Josh totally likes to fornicate with mortal women, and also apparently with the busty Undead, to judge by Delores.

I JUST FOUND MISS BARKER'S HAND IN
THE FRIDGE.

OKAY I WENT TO GET A GLASS OF WINE AND JUST AS I'M PUTTING THE WINE BACK I SEE THE PLASTIC TUPPERWARE CONTAINER, THE ONE THAT RYAN WAS CARRYING IN CHURCH JUST SITTING THERE ALL INNOCENT NEXT TO THE GHERKIN DIP AND I'M LIKE, WTF? SO I PEER AT IT A BIT CLOSER AND I CAN DEF SEE THAT THERE IS SOMETHING LURKING IN THERE NOT A TURTLE AND ALSO REEDS AND SHIT. SO I OPEN IT. AND THEN I CLOSE IT AGAIN REALLY QUICK.

I'M HIDING IN THE BEDROOM. IT'S STILL IN THE FRIDGE.

The thing that gets me most of all are those traces of Posh Pink nail polish. That just makes me sad. I mean it's repulsive and slimy and every time I open the Tupperware container, this wave of the foulest, most disgusting smell imaginable hits me almost enough to knock me out and I throw up. I've thrown up multiple times but I'm throwing up more out of sorrow than repulsion.

I actually said to it, 'I'm sorry.'

I said, 'I didn't know he was your fiancé.'

I said, 'I'm sorry this bad thing has happened to you.'

The fingers are all curled up, like a claw. And there are a few reeds in the container but she's not clutching them anymore. It's kind of like she's given up. It's sort of pathetic. What I've done now, just to be on the safe side, is I've jammed the whole container into the freezer. I figure that way she won't get active, like she did in church. I know you can pretty much euthanise crustaceans that way, so I'm hoping it's kind of humane.

Oh God, this is too weird.

There's this scratching sound, this horrible scratching scrabbling sound coming from the kitchen. It actually woke me up. I'm too scared to go and see what it is.

I should just go and check. I could be lying here in a pool of cold sweat for nothing.

OKAY, FUCK, IT IS COMING FROM THE FUCKING FREEZER!!!

I went into the kitchen and I'm standing there and, I swear to God, its scrabbling away inside the fucking freezer like it's trying to pick its way through the hinges or something. Very deliberate, very determined, working away very industriously. Every now and then it kind of throws itself against the inside of the freezer door like it's trying to push it open but it can't, so then it goes back to scrabbling away at the hinges. The more it scrabbles, the more frustrated and angry it gets, and then it throws itself at the freezer door again. I swear. I swear to God. I stood there for twenty minutes rooted to the spot just listening to it.

So what I've done is I've basically barricaded the entire fridge. I've piled up the two big armchairs one on top of the other directly in front of the fridge, then I upended the couch and heaved that against it.

Okay, so that was a bad idea. Now it's literally hurling itself repeatedly against the inside of the freezer door in a blind rage. I am beginning to think it might actually manage to push it open because it seems to be getting stronger and heavier, maybe as it freezes up. I'm thinking all I can do is move all the furniture out of the way, and somehow try to tip the fridge face down. There is no way the little fucker will get out then.

----

tipping the fridge over a complete fucking diasater because as I tip the angry little motherfucker throws itself against the door and the freezer door swings open and the hand drops out and scarbbles away quickly just in time to avoid being flattened by the fridge. I just fucking lose it run to the front door but it's all bolte dup and while I'm desperately trying to slide across all those locks Miss Barker's hand has hold of my ankle now I swear and I'm beating it off with an umbrella I'm thinking fuck it's ging to rip my foot off finally I get the door open and I try to wrench the hand off my foot wjich is tricky due to how slimy then I fling it as hard as I can against the wall and I bolt out of there to the car I jump in the car and the fucker wont start and I'm screaming to my father dad dad help me please help me and the engine suddenly turns over an dthats it I'm out f here I'm out of town

----

Do you believe in angels? I totally do. I believe my father swooped down from heaven and with supernatural strength lifted my car in his arms and carried it to the Ridge. Why? Because he saw I was in trouble. Because he wanted me back with him.

At first I was surprised to find myself at the Ridge. My intention, I thought, was to drive myself out of town, which seemed the logical course of action given my predicament. But instead my father deposited me at the Ridge, and for a while I just sat there in calm reflection, watching the dawn break. After the harrowing night I'd had, I felt strangely at peace. More than peace; I felt an almost euphoric oneness with myself and my place in the universe.

After a while, I got out of the car and sat on my usual rock and even tried to meditate a little. I had this feeling that, after the horrors of last night, a kind of 'reset' button had been pressed, and maybe I could start afresh. But as the first glimmers of the sun began to peek over the mountains, I noticed that my feeling of oneness with the universe was beginning to dissipate (surprise, surprise), and instead I began to experience sharp pangs of intense loneliness combined with a dull ache of gnawing anxiety. It felt imperative that I talk to someone in the real world. So I called Doc.

I guess I must have woken him, because he sounded different, a little groggy. He didn't even seem to know who I was at first, and when he finally realised, he apologised and said he had a couple of Eleanors these days and sometimes he got us mixed up. At first I felt a stab of jealousy: who were these other cancer-ravaged Eleanors that he tended to and how did their tumours compare to mine? And then I felt a wave of sadness at the never-ending tide of women such as myself, with their mutilated breasts and their radiation burns, turning their faces to Doc as I turned mine to the sun this morning, hoping for some kind of salvation. And the terrible pity of this image made me weep, and for a moment I couldn't utter a word.

'Eleanor?' he said.

'I love you,' I said. 'That's all. I love you.'

There was silence on the other end of the line, and I panicked. I realised how unhinged I must seem, ringing him at five in the morning with weepy declarations of love. And so, in a bid to sound less unhinged, I told him how grateful I was for the wonderful work he did, not just for me but for all these other tumour-infested Eleanors, and how I'd simply felt compelled to ring him up and tell him so.

'That's really sweet of you, Eleanor,' said Doc, and in the background, I could hear a female voice complaining about being woken at this hour. That would be Mrs Doc. I've seen a photo of her on his desk. She has the sinewy look of someone who plays a lot of tennis, but apparently she's some kind of high-flying immunologist. Whenever I ask after her, which is never, she's always at some conference in Prague or Boston or Paris.

'But how are you anyway? How's the new job?' he asks. I can hear the sound of rapid typing on a keyboard, and I realise he must have moved into another room and be blearily checking my file on his computer.

'It's okay.'

'Have you got a cold? Your voice sounds different.'

'No. Well, maybe. Just a bit of a croak.'

'And how's your twinging going? Your breast twinging?'

'It's still there,' I say. 'It's getting worse.'

'Are you taking your tamoxifen?'

'No. I stopped.'

'What? Why? Why did you do that?'

'I thought I was pregnant.'

'I see.'

'But it turns out I'm not, so it doesn't matter.'

There's a moment of silence on the other end. And I guess, looking back, there may have been the sound of twigs breaking underfoot, or a sudden whiff of pine and crushed spearmint in the air. But as usual, I guess I wasn't paying enough attention.

'Well, I can understand you must be feeling pretty sad about that,' Doc is saying. 'But from my point of view, with where you are health-wise, it's probably for the best right now.'

'He's wrong,' says Gregory. 'Health-wise, for you, it's not very good at all.'

I don't know where he sprung from. He was just there all of a sudden, standing right in front of me, looking unbelievably pissed off.

'Can you pass me your phone, please?' he asks, holding out his hand.

He looks in no mood to be argued with, so I pass him my phone, whereupon he tosses it into the Reservoir. As it falls through the air, I can hear Doc's tiny disembodied voice going, '*Eleanor? Are you there? Eleanor?*' He's too far away to help me now. The water is such a long way down I barely hear the splash.

'What did I say to you, Eleanor?' says Gregory in a weary tone, like I have been sorely testing his patience.

'I can't remember,' I say, which is true. But clearly it's the wrong answer because now he gets even more irritated. He furrows his brow and digs his hands deep into the pockets of his pants, like he's trying to decide how best to deal with me. Only then do I take a moment, and I glance around and realise that, of all the stupid places I could possibly be standing, I'm actually right on the edge of the precipice! How I got to be right on the edge, I do not know, but it spooks the bejesus out of me. I look down, which was a very bad idea—straight away I wish I hadn't. Because down below is the water, soft and inviting as a chenille bedspread, and all at once I feel that pull, that beckoning, like the bus with its door open. I'm woozy. My head's swimming. I start to teeter back and forth like one of those kids' toys—it would almost be comical except it's not. It's actually quite alarming. I'm thinking, Wow, all this teetering, is this some kind of metaphor for Life? Funny the things that pop into your head! Because the fact is, I need to grab hold of something but there's nothing to grab hold of. Gregory is no help—he doesn't even seem to notice my predicament. He's too busy pontificating about the universe and the stars and the trees and his disappointment in my fecundity, and at some point he makes a gesture (I guess to reinforce a point or something?), but anyway it startles me and I realise I am no longer teetering but instead I'm falling backwards over the edge.

It's an odd feeling—not entirely unpleasurable—weightless and surreal and almost in some small way *liberating*. I mean, liberating in the realisation that all connection has been lost with terra firma, and with it all the workaday cares and worries that are associated with terra firma. But in that knowledge there is also terror, and then out of nowhere comes a desperate hopeless imperative to *reconnect* somehow, no matter what. Let me say, it's not a dignified thing. In my case, as I'm falling, I keep trying to grab hold of these clumps of long grass that are growing out of the side of the cliff face, and believe it or not, I actually succeed in clutching hold of one. I hang there for a second or two and (hope springs eternal!) I remember thinking, Phew, that was close! But then the clump of grass pulls right out of the cliff face, roots and all, and I realise, *This is it, I'm a goner, I'm going to die like Miss Barker.*

I was underwater for a while, and it was cold and very murky.
I can hold my breath for a long time so I wasn't particularly
worried about that. I was more concerned about becoming
entangled in something, or having one of my panic attacks.
But oddly enough, on this occasion I felt a tremendous sense
of calm and equanimity. My feeling of oneness with the universe had returned to me. I looked up and I saw these duck
feet paddling above me, and the song leapt into my mind: *Old
mother duckie, and her little duckies nine.* These little guys have
no idea I'm lurking down below, and I'm tempted to yank
one of the ducklings underwater, like an eel, just to see the
surprised look on its face. I don't, of course, but the thought
of it makes me giggle.

I let the gentle current float me downstream for a while, then,
when I reach the township, I wade out of the water through
the sludge, and I trudge home. I'm feeling tired now, and
very cold, and my bones are sore, probably from the fall. I
can see the children heading off to school, and I'm surprised,
because I have that feeling you get like it's a Saturday or the
holidays or something. Briefly, I think, Oh, gee, should I be

teaching? And then I remember that they sacked me, and as a matter of fact, I feel relieved.

Because I'm going home. That's my plan. By which I mean, getting the hell out of this place, like I've tried before. As I turn into the driveway, I see my little Corolla waiting loyally for me, and it's such a comforting sight, I smile. I dig into my damp pocket and find my keys, and as I clamber into the driver's seat, I'm overwhelmed by the lovely stuffy way it smells of old vinyl upholstery and the long-ago residue of Dad's cigarettes. I reach out and touch the St Christopher medallion, just for luck. Then, as a precaution, I push down the locks on all the doors. I even check under the sun visor, just to be sure that Miss Barker's hand isn't lurking up there like a spider.

It takes a few attempts to get the car started, and for a moment there I lose my newfound equanimity and I scream, '*Come on, come on, don't fuck with me!*' But at last it sputters into life, and I put my foot on the accelerator to give it some juice. It revs reassuringly. 'We're outta here,' I say to my father, who is sitting beside me now, and I reverse out of the driveway, sideswiping one of the gateposts.

'Check your mirrors next time,' says my dad. 'And maybe take it a little slower.'

'Okay, okay,' I say, chuckling, and then I glance at myself in the rear-view mirror. I look a fright. My hair is all matted

with duck feathers, and I have the strung-out look of someone who hasn't slept in a while. Oh well, I think to myself.
Nothing a good night's sleep and some shampoo and condi-
tioner won't fix. Maybe we'll stay in a motel tonight.

'Can you wind your window up?' I ask my dad. 'I'm cold.'

'In a minute,' says Dad, because he's sucking on one of his
Marlboro Lights.

We wind through a couple of back streets and then turn on
to the main road that leads out of town. I put my foot to the
floor, and a feeling of exhilaration overwhelms me. I glance
down at the speedometer. The needle is moving past eighty,
then ninety, then a hundred, a hundred and twenty.

'What's the speed limit here?' asks Dad.

'I don't give a fuck,' I respond.

'You'll give a fuck if you get a ticket,' says Dad, and I glance
at him in surprise because it's not like him to swear. He
catches my look and he grins at me, a bit embarrassed, and
then we both start laughing because, let's face it, the whole
situation is so insane! And just at that moment, as I'm rounding the last curve before the highway, I see a cop car tucked
away on the verge and Senior Sergeant Saunders pointing a
radar gun at me.

'Pull over, pull over,' says Dad.

I mean, *please.*

I cannot catch a break.

The thing is, I probably wouldn't have pulled over if it wasn't for Dad, but Dad's always been terrified of offending anyone he sees as an authority figure. So I pull over like a dutiful daughter, and Senior Sergeant Saunders ambles over and leans in my window.

'Why are you in such a hurry?' he asks. 'You realise you were fifty clicks over the speed limit? Blow into this, please.'

And he passes me a breathalyser. For fuck's sake! Not that I'm really worried, because as far as I can remember I haven't been drinking. So I blow into it and I hand it back to him.

'That's funny,' he says, staring at it. He gives it a shake. 'Try again. Blow harder this time.'

So I try again. He frowns. Then he goes through the whole performance. He stares at it. He shakes it. He taps it. Then he shows me the digital read-out. Two digital E's flashing on and off.

'Error message,' says Saunders. 'Which is weird. I tested it just before.'

He blows into it now himself. This time, a reading comes up: .006.

'See?' he says. 'Works fine for me. You must have the lungs of a kitten.'

'Actually, I have phenomenal lung capacity,' I tell him. 'I have the lungs of a free diver.'

'Well, try again then.' He wipes the mouthpiece with his hand, and passes it back to me. 'Really give it some grunt this time.'

So I blow again as hard as I can, but up comes the error message. What does this mean? Am I dead or something??

'Well, regardless,' says Saunders, 'given the speed you were travelling, I've got no choice but to cancel your licence on the spot.'

'*What??*' I cry.

'Hand over your keys,' he says, 'and get out of the car.'

I can't believe it. I seriously can't believe it. I turn to my dad, and I actually say, 'Can you believe this???' But he has his head down and he's pretending to study a map—conflict avoidance, his usual pattern. I'd forgotten how weak he can be, and I'm irritated. So I get out of the car and I slam the door as hard as I can in a pointed fashion, then I fling the keys at Saunders.

'You can have it,' I say. 'It's a shit box.'

I start trudging up the road. Because I'm still getting out of here, Dad or no Dad. Nothing and nobody is going to stop me. I'll hitchhike if I have to; I don't care if I'm gang-raped and murdered and chopped into a thousand little pieces—that would actually be preferable to staying a moment longer in this hellhole. And as I'm stomping along and muttering to myself, I suddenly become aware of this rumbling rattling sound and these noxious horrible fumes, and I glance up and I see this bus, this dirty grey bus, coming straight towards me. My heart jolts with sudden hope. I actually feel so hopeful I could burst into song. Because of course I'd forgotten about the bus, the bus on Thursday. I run directly towards it, waving my arms, and next thing I hear this hoarse asthmatic squeal as it slams on its

FLEET

To buy any of our books and to find out
more about Fleet, our authors and titles, as well
as events and book clubs, visit our website

www.littlebrown.co.uk

and follow us on Twitter

@FleetReads
@LittleBrownUK